MAVERICK

IRON ROGUES MC

FIONA DAVENPORT

MAVERICK

Maverick Crawford knew that Molly Mackenzie was off limits. She was too young for him...and a Silver Saints MC princess. Her protective father was their president, so starting anything with Molly would cause trouble between their clubs.

But that didn't stop Maverick from taking her straight out of their tattoo parlor and claiming her for himself. Only someone wanted the feisty redhead to belong to them instead.

PROLOGUE
MOLLY

Growing up in the Silver Saints MC was way different from what outsiders assumed. When my dad fell for my mom, the club became all about family, one that continued to grow over the years. To the point where there were so many kids that it made sense to do a combined birthday for a bunch of them at the clubhouse today.

I had three siblings of my own, but I loved having a ton of bonus cousins who were related to me by choice instead of blood. Although I was more of an aunt to this crew since I was sixteen years older than them. Not that our age difference held me back from playing with them when I got the chance. Which was why I had volunteered to organize the games for all of them today.

"Okay, guys! Who wants to play tag?" I called, grabbing everyone's attention except for Britta.

Lee and Kansas's daughter had recently turned nine and was one of the guests of honor for the birthday party. Instead of running toward me with almost everyone else, she raced toward the back door of the clubhouse and threw herself at the guy who'd just walked outside.

I thought I knew everyone connected to the club enough to be invited to family events, but I didn't recognize him. And if we'd met before, I definitely would've met him since he was pretty damn unforgettable. He was tall and muscular with dark auburn hair that my fingers itched to comb through, and piercing blue eyes that crinkled at the corners as he crouched down to greet Britta.

I was too far away to read what was written on the cut he was wearing, but Britta had solved the mystery of who he was when she had cried, "Uncle Mav!"

Maverick Crawford was the VP of the Iron Rogues and Kansas's older brother. His club was back in the town where she grew up, and his introduction to the Silver Saints had been a rough one since he kidnapped Lorelei, Grey's old lady. From the gossip I'd heard back then, he hadn't been happy with Kansas's relationship with Lee and wanted to make a statement by taking his sister. Only he hadn't known that a Silver Saint had claimed Lorelei.

Luckily, no harm had come to Lorelei, and Maverick had come to terms with his sister being with Lee. Although it had all worked out in the end, I was pretty sure this was the first time he'd ever visited the Silver Saints compound. With how my body reacted to him from afar, my dad would probably regret extending the invitation.

Even surrounded by a bunch of kids who were excited to play tag, my gaze kept straying toward Maverick. Britta had dragged him over to Kansas and Lorelei before tugging on his hand and begging, "Come play tag, Uncle Mav! Pleeeeeease!"

Callum, Cash and Karina's oldest, ran up and grabbed his other hand. "Yeah, play with us, Uncle Mav!!"

Maverick's deep laughter drifted toward me as he shot his sister an amused smile and shrugged. "Lead the way. But don't come crying to your mommas when I kick your butts."

The kids giggled and took off. Maverick waited half a minute to give them a good head start, then chased them.

I'd been so focused on him that I missed

Grayson, Lorelei and Grey's son, coming at me. I fell to the ground as he tackled me and yelled, "Tag! You're it!"

I hadn't gone down too hard, but it took me a moment to stop laughing. When I looked up, Maverick stood over me with his hand stretched out. I slid my palm against his, and it felt as though I was touching a live wire with how all of my nerve endings came to life.

After he helped me up, I just gawked up at him, trying to catch my breath. Acutely aware of the fact that we were surrounded by men who still saw me as a little girl even though I was twenty-five years old, I knew that I needed to do something to break the sensual spell between us before one of them noticed my reaction to him. So I poked him in the chest and yelled, "Tag! You're it!"

Then I sprinted toward a copse of trees where many of the kids had already found hiding spots. I had barely made it to my hiding spot before he gave chase. When he got close, I bit my lip to hold back my soft laughter but not before a giggle trickled out.

"Fair warning, baby," he growled as he prowled closer. "When I catch you, I'm not going to let you go."

My lips curved into a grin. "What makes you think you'll be able to catch me?"

Silence was my only answer, which only made me more confident that he wouldn't be able to find me.

Staring down at the ground beneath the tree branch I was perched on, I was disappointed not to see a sign of him. "Giving up already?"

Before I knew what was happening, the branch gave out beneath me, and I tumbled straight into Maverick's arms. Stunned that he'd been able to creep up behind me, I blinked up at him in shock. Then he winked, and my cheeks filled with heat.

"I win," he growled, his lips curving into a smile that had butterflies swarming in my belly.

I smirked back at him. "So it seems, Maverick."

He quirked a brow. "You know my name, so it's only fair that you tell me yours."

"Molly MacKenzie," I murmured, hoping that the knowledge of who my father was wouldn't scare him off like it did with most men.

The heat in his intense blue eyes didn't dim, but he did set me on my feet, which turned out to be a good thing. My dad's daughter radar must've gone off because he marched through the trees toward us before anything else could be said. His gaze darted between us, and a muscle jumped in his jaw when he saw how close we were standing.

Pointing at the branch on the ground right next to us, I muttered, "You should be thanking Maverick for catching me instead of glaring at him."

"And he should be hunting down the hiding spots of one of the kids so they don't get bored with the game instead of looking for you," my dad retorted, crossing his arms over his chest.

"Already know exactly where my niece is hiding." Maverick jerked his chin at my dad. "Was planning on tagging her next."

"Good."

My shoulder slumped when the sexy biker stomped off in the direction Britta had run. "Did you come out here to ruin my fun, or were you planning on playing too?"

"Stay away from Maverick. He's the VP of another club and a decade older than you," my dad growled.

Considering what happened when my parents got together and their age gap, he was being incredibly hypocritical right now. "At least he didn't kidnap me like you did with Mom."

"And he'd better not." My dad's eyes narrowed as he stared holes into Maverick's back. "We let him get away with that shit once, but being Kansas's big brother won't save him if he dares to mess with you."

I had no doubt that my dad meant what he said... but that didn't stop me from wishing that Maverick wouldn't heed the warning he'd just been given.

1

MAVERICK

A sane person would probably be second-guessing themselves when contemplating what I was about to do. But I'd been going crazy since the moment I laid eyes on Molly Mackenzie— the oldest daughter of Jared "Mac" Mackenzie, the president of the Silver Saints Motorcycle Club.

They had a fierce reputation, and not many people were brave enough to go against them. It wasn't much different from the rep my own MC, the Iron Rogues, had in our territory. And if my dad— who'd been the first VP—saw some older punk sniffing around his daughter, he'd have warned him off too. Which was exactly what I'd done when I found out about Lee and Kansas. Then the shit hit the fan when I took his sister for a trade, and when everything finally calmed down, our clubs had a truce and loose connection.

Now, I was about to jeopardize everything. Still...I felt no hesitation.

Ever since the birthday party two weeks ago, I'd been racking my brain, trying to figure out how to see Molly again. She was well guarded since she was not only a club princess but also the first daughter. Although, considering the wide berth her protection gave her, I was pretty sure she wasn't aware of them.

I'd been hoping to devise a way to see her that wouldn't send up red flags and give me time with her before I had her dad trying to put me in the ground. But after two weeks of missing her, waking up in a sweat from dirty dreams, and biting my brothers' heads off because I was always in a shit mood, I'd come to the conclusion that there was no subtle way of doing this.

I'd also spent the past couple of weeks learning everything I could about Molly and her life. She was a tattoo artist—one of the most highly sought after in the area. Silver Ink, where she worked, always had a waiting list. She was really fucking talented, and I was determined to have her stamp on me. So this seemed like the easiest way to see her again without alerting the cavalry right off the bat.

I hopped off my Harley and strode toward the entrance to the tattoo parlor. It was attached to the SS compound on the back, but the front entrance was public, so I didn't have to deal with as much security.

A little bell dinged when I walked inside and pulled off my shades, sticking them in the inner pocket of my cut. The place had an edgy, rock n' roll vibe that was kick-ass, with black floors that had silver flecks, dark gray walls, and black leather furniture. There was shiny chrome all over the place, though, and bright lights, so the place didn't seem dark. The walls were also covered with metal artwork that looked like they had probably been drawings for custom ink.

Behind a front desk were a series of tattoo stations, all separated with curtains in case the client wanted privacy. I froze when I saw a gorgeous redhead sitting with her back to me, leaning over the arm of a client as she worked. Tendrils of jealousy snaked their way through my body, and I clenched my fists at my side.

Get a fucking grip, Mav.

The guy was at least fifty, had a gray handlebar mustache, and a bit of a beer belly. It wasn't like he was competition. However, it was when he hissed and blinked up at the ceiling, clearly trying not to cry, that those feelings disappeared.

"Can I help you?"

Suppressing a laugh, I smoothed my expression as I turned my focus to the girl behind the front desk. When she smiled, I immediately knew she was related to my woman. They had the same lips and eye color, though this girl's hair was a darker auburn, and she had fewer freckles. Molly's sister Dahlia did piercings at Silver Ink, so I assumed she was the one who greeted me.

Tearing my eyes away from my woman, I ambled up to the counter. "Got an appointment."

"Hi. I'm Dahlia. You must be M. Crawford," the girl said as she typed something on the computer.

"Yeah." While I was willing to deal with whatever shit blew my way over claiming Molly, I figured it best not to send up any red flags just yet. So I'd made the appointment under just my first initial and last name.

"I see it's your first time with us, but clearly, this isn't your first tattoo." She gestured to my neck. Most of it was covered in ink, as well as a string of words across my collarbone, and a lot of it was visible above the crew neck of my white T-shirt.

She leaned over the counter a little, and I lifted

my chin to give her a better view. "That's really nice work," she murmured with surprise, her eyes coming back up to mine.

My ink had all been done by one of my brothers, Whiskey, who ran Iron Inkworks, the tattoo shop owned by our club. Whiskey was one of the best artists I'd ever met, but after doing some research and seeing Molly's work, I was looking forward to having her stamp on me for multiple reasons.

"Did your artist retire or something?" Dahlia asked as she grabbed a clipboard with a sheet of paper attached and a pen. "He's obviously very good."

"Molly's better," I replied gruffly, taking the proffered clipboard.

She smiled smugly. "Yeah, she is."

I filled out the paperwork while she went into a little spiel for new customers. When she finished, I handed it back, and she motioned toward a waiting area.

"Have a seat. Molly's just finishing up. It shouldn't be more than ten minutes."

I nodded and walked over to a chair that gave me a view of the working area so that when I sat down, I still had eyes on Molly.

Less than a minute later, the front door opened,

and two people entered the studio. The man and woman were both attractive, young—probably early twenties—and were holding hands.

"Hey, Dahlia!" the woman said brightly as she approached the desk.

"Fawn!" Dahlia smiled happily, but when the man lifted the hand he was holding to show off a sparkling diamond on his girl's finger, she screeched and ran around the desk to hug Fawn. "You're engaged!"

The girls laughed and hugged while the man stood back and watched his fiancée with a soft expression.

"Congratulations, Dale," Dahlia effused, giving him a quick hug. Then she hopped back and gasped. "Does this mean...?"

Fawn rolled her eyes, but she shifted nervously on her feet. "A deal's a deal. Do you have time to do it?"

Dahlia clapped her hands and bounced on her toes. "Of course!" Then she put her hand on Fawn's shoulder and smiled reassuringly. "Relax, girl. You know I've got this."

Fawn sighed and turned to her fiancé with narrowed eyes. "You're still holding up our end of the deal, right?"

"Absolutely," he assured her with a firm jerk of his chin before sliding an arm around her waist and pulling her close.

Dahlia grinned and dropped her voice as they continued talking, but their conversation still floated to my ears. I only paid it half attention because I was keeping an eye on Molly.

"Dale, do you know which piercing you're getting?" Dahlia asked. Fawn's face flushed, and her eyes dropped to the ground, though there was an upward curve to her lips.

Dale's cheeks turned slightly red. "Um...since I picked the VCH for Fawn, she wants...um...a Prince Albert for me."

"And the tattoo?"

I stopped paying them any attention when Molly suddenly sat back and set her tattoo machine on the little table beside her. She cleaned up the guy's tattoo and treated it, finally covering it with gauze. They both stood, and I was mesmerized by Molly's graceful fluidity. And I got a little lost in the sight of her perfect ass encased in a pair of tight leather pants. Her red curls were pulled up and piled on top of her head, showing off the Silver Ink logo on the back of her black tank top.

She took off a pair of gloves and dropped them

into a trash can before walking beside her client to the front. My pants were already tight from how sexy she looked from behind, but seeing her big tits, slender neck, and drop-fucking-gorgeous face made my cock hard as steel. Shifting in my seat, I did my best to hide my reaction.

"You know the drill, Buck," she told the old guy with a smile. "I'll tell Phyllis you didn't cry this time."

Buck glared at her, but there was no real menace in it, or I'd have been between them with my hand around his throat before he could take his next breath. "She wouldn't believe you," he finally said with a sigh, making Molly chuckle.

"Molly," Dahlia interrupted. "Your next appointment is here." Before Molly could turn in my direction, her sister put her hand on her arm and tipped her chin toward the couple. "Fawn and Dale are here to 'seal the deal,'" she finished with a giggle.

Molly congratulated them with hugs, making me grit my teeth when the little punk put an arm around her. Even though it was brief and he didn't linger.

I cleared my throat as I stood, and finally, those emerald-green orbs were trained on me once more.

"Maverick," she breathed, eyes widening as she recognized me.

I didn't bother to answer, just smiled and winked.

"What are you doing here?" she asked, and I cocked an eyebrow. There was only one reason I would be at Silver Ink, and she was smart enough to know what it was.

With sure strides, I closed the distance between us and grunted, "I warned you, I'd catch you, baby."

"Molly?" Dahlia's tone was hesitant as she looked between us. "Is everything okay? Should I call Dad?"

Molly's head whipped toward her sister, and she groaned. "For the love of all that is holy, do *not* call Dad. Good grief, Dahls, I can handle my own shit."

Her sister didn't say anything else, but she continued to watch us closely.

"Do you know what you want?" Molly queried, watching me curiously.

"I know exactly what I fucking want, princess."

She double blinked, then inhaled sharply. "Okay, let's go to my station, and you can show me—"

"Wait," Dahlia interrupted again, making me want to put duct tape over her mouth. "You're done for the day after..."

"Maverick," Molly supplied when her sister paused.

"Right. Anyway, do you think you might want to stick around and do Dale's tat?"

I repressed a sigh, getting really fucking impatient with sharing my woman's attention, but I didn't want to come on any stronger than I already was, so I swallowed my irritation.

"Sure. You're still doing the same design?" Molly asked Dale.

He nodded, then grabbed the hem of his shirt and raised it, revealing far too much of a ripped stomach since his jeans were hanging around his hips. "We decided to put it here," he said, pointing at a spot that was so low on the right side, it couldn't have been but mere centimeters from the guy's junk.

The weeks of frustration at not seeing her, then all this bullshit at the shop, and now this guy wanting my woman to basically ink his dick took me to the end of my rope.

"Not a fucking chance in hell," I growled. "No fucking way am I letting you anywhere near my woman."

Molly gasped and swung around to face me, putting her hands on her hips, looking unbelievably fuckable. "You can't just—"

Fuck it. I was so done with this bullshit. Before anyone realized what was happening, I bent over and put my shoulder in her stomach as I wrapped an arm around her legs.

"What are you doing?" Molly shrieked, wiggling frantically.

"NOW should I call Dad?" Dahlia yelled.

I slapped Molly's ass and muttered, "Calm down before you hurt yourself."

"No!" I wasn't sure if she was talking to me or Dahlia, and I didn't give a shit. I was already headed for the door.

"I'll deal with this," she snapped. "Cover for me for a few days."

I grinned since no one could see my face.

"Fine. But you better call me every freaking day to let me know you're alive!"

I stomped out to my bike and set Molly on the back of it, caging her between my spread thighs while I dug a helmet and my leather jacket out of my saddle bag for her. Once I put them both on her, I gave her a stern look. "Stay."

Molly opened her mouth, most likely to say something sassy that would only make me want to fuck her even more. So I captured her lips to shut her up. But I had to rip my mouth away almost immediately or the only place we'd be going was to the nearest hotel. And I didn't want that to give Molly the wrong impression of what was happening right now.

This wasn't a fling, a one-night stand, or any kind of temporary relationship.

I was staking my claim.

2

MOLLY

I'd ridden on the back of my dad's bike plenty of times, but being behind Maverick was a totally different experience. A big part of the reason I stayed put for the two-hour ride to the Iron Rogues compound was because of how much I enjoyed the feel of his big body between my legs. As he pulled through the gates, I realized that I must've been more like my mom than I thought because I'd just assisted in my own kidnapping. And pulled my sister into the situation since I'd asked her to cover for me.

When Maverick killed the engine, I yanked the helmet off my head and handed it to him. Then I slid off his bike and shrugged off his jacket, tossing it at him as well. Glaring, I planted my fists on my hips.

"You could've warned me that we were going all the way to Old Bridge."

"Where else was I going to take you, princess?" He toed down the kickstand and climbed off his motorcycle. "I wouldn't have anyone to take my back if we'd gone elsewhere." He stowed the helmet and jacket in his saddlebags, then faced me.

"Maybe you shouldn't have kidnapped me if you're so worried about it," I quipped, arching my brow as he stepped closer.

Wrapping his large hand around my arm, he smirked at me. "Didn't say I was worried about the price I'm gonna have to pay for taking you."

His confidence only made him sexier, but his reply left me confused. As he tugged me toward the clubhouse, I asked, "Then why was it so important to have your club brothers at your back?"

"Because you're with me." He paused at the door and lifted his other hand to swipe his thumb down my cheek. "And I'm not going to take any risks when it comes to your safety."

I'd always pictured myself with a guy who was fearless and protective, and each minute I spent with Maverick made me wonder if he was the one I'd been waiting for. Not only was I wildly attracted to him, but he also kept doing stuff that reminded me of how the men I'd grown up with treated their wives. Something he reinforced only minutes after he led me inside the Iron Rogues clubhouse.

One of his club brothers glanced over his shoulder at us, then swiveled on his barstool and stuck two fingers in his mouth to let out a loud whistle. "Damn, Mav. You been waiting for the hottest chick you could find to finally bring one around to the clubhouse?"

Maverick's body went solid before he shrugged off his cut and shoved my arms in the holes. Well aware of the meaning behind that move—and loving that he'd never brought another woman to the compound—a delicious shiver raced up my spine. But if I was going to wear Maverick's name on my back, I didn't want it to be because of a knee-jerk reflex. Since I only planned on giving myself to one man, he needed to put more thought into the action.

Especially when I wasn't completely sure what his motive was for taking me from Silver Ink. There was no mistaking the desire in his blue orbs when he looked at me, so I knew he wanted me. But there was a huge jump between temporary lust and forever—and I hadn't waited this long just for a quick roll between the sheets.

I slipped the leather vest off my shoulders and

handed it back to him. "If you're giving this to me for protection, I don't need it. My dad made sure that I know how to take care of myself. And I shouldn't need to worry about my safety while I'm here, right? That was the whole point of you bringing me to your compound?"

His knuckles went white as he clenched his cut. "What if I have a different reason for wanting you to have my name on you?"

Considering the roadblocks my dad would put in our way if we decided to be together, "if" wasn't good enough. He needed to be ready for the fight he would have on his hands. "If you're gonna claim me, it will be the right way. Not a spur-of-the-moment decision made out of jealousy."

"Shit, she's sassy too?" The other guy beamed a flirtatious smile at me. "You're fiery like your red hair, huh? Just my kind of woman."

Maverick stepped in front of me, blocking my view of his club brother. "Keep your eyes off her and your mouth shut, Pike."

"C'mon, man. I didn't mean any harm," Pike mumbled. "But you gotta admit the girl is even hotter when she's being feisty."

I bit my lip to hold back a giggle, wondering if this guy was being serious or if he was just having fun pushing Maverick's buttons. I'd been old enough when several of the Silver Saints had found their old ladies to see how much fun the other guys had giving them a hard time. And Maverick was reacting pretty much the same way...which gave me hope that he'd taken me for the same reason Dax had taken Arya when I was eight. Kidnapping your future old lady was a long-standing tradition in the Silver Saints, but I liked his motive for it the most—he hadn't wanted to wait another minute to claim his woman.

"I know you heard me tell you to keep your mouth shut about her." Maverick shoved his cut back onto his shoulders and strode toward the bar.

Heaving a deep sigh, I glanced around the Iron Rogues clubhouse and compared it to the one I'd grown up in. Both had a large space where all of the guys could hang out, but there was none of the homey vibe that ours had, and I wondered if that was because none of their leadership had old ladies. I'd heard enough stories growing up to know that the vibe of the Silver Saints had changed when my dad fell for my mom, and that the club turned into more of a family as each member fell in love and had children.

The Iron Rogues clubhouse was utterly masculine without any hint of a feminine touch. Kind of like a big bachelor pad with black leather couches, a pool table, a poker table, and several big-screen televisions. The red leather stools lining the bar were the only pop of color in the dark room.

Pike slid off the one he'd been sitting on, his hands held palms up in a gesture of surrender. "I hear you, man. I'll keep my eyes off your girl and my mouth shut about her from now on."

"You can do one better for me." Maverick returned to my side. "Spread the word with our brothers and any hangers-on that they need to watch themselves because Molly Mackenzie is here, and she's off-limits."

I snickered and blinked up at him as innocently as I could manage. "I thought you wanted your guys to help keep an eye on me while I was here?"

The growl that rumbled up his wide chest made my panties damp. Judging by the knowing look in his eyes as he nudged me toward a set of stairs at the other side of the room, I hadn't been able to hide my reaction to him.

"Good luck with her," Pike muttered. "I have a feeling you're gonna need it."

Maverick just sighed as he led me up to what I assumed was his room. When got to his door, I leaned against the wall as he opened it. "I know I didn't put up much of a fight when you kidnapped me from Silver Ink, but heading straight for your room as soon as you bring me here is way out of character for me."

He mirrored my position on the other side of the door, grinning at me. "Is it really kidnapping if you were willing to let me take you?"

"Probably not." I shook my head with a soft laugh. "My personality is a lot more like my dad's, but I must get that part from my mom."

He cocked his head to the side, his brows drawing together. "What do you mean?"

"There was stuff going down between the Silver Saints and my grandfather's club, the Hounds of Hellfire, back when my parents got together," I explained, my lips curving into a smile as I recalled all the times I'd been told about their meet cute. "My dad needed my grandpa to do something, so he decided to take my mom. Only when he showed up at their clubhouse to kidnap her, she literally provided the ladder they used to climb out her window."

Maverick's eyes widened. "Damn, that was ballsy as fuck, on both their parts."

"Luckily, they managed to work everything out, even though my dad and grandpa are both stubborn as all get-out. Especially when it comes to protecting the people they love." Tapping my foot on the floor, I quirked a brow. "Which doesn't bode well for you, but at least the Iron Rogues aren't my father's rival MC."

"We are now. Because my VP is a fucking idiot."

My head whipped around at the deep grumble, and I gawked at the man stomping down the hallway toward us. The president of the Iron Rogues MC was here...and he didn't look the least bit happy.

3

MAVERICK

"You lost your fucking mind, Mav?" Kye "Fox" Pearson, my prez, snarled in a deadly tone. He started to say something else, then stopped as his gaze went to my woman. He growled and shot another glare in my direction before snapping, "My office. Now." Then he whipped around and stomped down the hall.

Sighing, I unlocked my door and put my hand on Molly's lower back to gently guide her inside. Like the Silver Saints, the Iron Rogues had a compound for the main clubhouse, lodge, and offices. However, rather than several of our businesses being attached to the property or scattered through town, we owned most of the buildings in a two-block radius on all four sides, creating a sort of "neighborhood."

Our clubhouse wasn't as big as some, but that was because many buildings had apartments above them, with a kitchen, bathroom, common area, and a few bedrooms. Some rooms had their own bathroom, usually given to brothers who lived on our property full time.

Fox and I both lived in the clubhouse, one of us on each end. Our rooms were the largest—more like a small one-bedroom apartment without a kitchenette since we all ate in the main clubhouse kitchen.

I shut the door to my room behind me and pointed at the first door on my left. "Bedroom and bathroom through there. Feel free to hang out and watch TV, nap, take a shower, whatever you want. Long as you don't leave this room."

She looked as though she was about to argue, so I hooked her around the waist and hauled her close so I could plant a quick, hard kiss on her lips. "Fuck," I grunted when I pulled away. "Gotta stop doing that shit. Next time we kiss, I'm gonna take my time because after just those small tastes, I'm already addicted."

Molly blinked up at me, her green pools a little glassy, making me smirk. I patted her ass, then kissed the tip of her nose before releasing her. "Won't be long. Be good."

The confrontation with Fox wasn't unexpected, but that didn't mean I wasn't pissed as fuck to be pulled away from my woman. Still, I knew my place, so by the time I got downstairs and entered his office, I was much calmer.

Fox sat behind a desk, one you'd expect to see in the executive's office of a financier on Wall Street— big, modern, with multiple monitors and nothing out of place. He was a neat freak, a complete nerd, and the most badass motherfucker I'd ever met.

We'd pretty much been born best friends, even though Fox was three years older than me. My dad had been the Iron Rogue's VP before me, and Fox's dad was prez before him. The club was our legacy, and we'd grown up knowing that, but before we patched and were given our road names, we were just Kye and Mav. My dad always said he gave me my road name at birth, and everyone agreed when the day came to take mine on.

I played soccer and became a master at several different styles of martial arts. I was already an excellent shot when I signed up for the National Guard. I served eight years and got a degree in business because I knew it would be an asset to me when I took over as VP.

Kye was just as athletic and deadly, but he was also wicked smart and had a head for numbers. He went to college for finance and then worked on Wall Street for a few years. He wasn't just brilliant; he was wily—which was how he eventually got the moniker Fox—and made several million before getting bored and coming home. He patched years before I did, working as treasurer until becoming the president.

Neither of us expected to be stepping into our roles so early in life, but my mom somehow talked my dad into retiring and traveling the world on their bikes. Fox's mom had died when he was a teenager, so we thought his dad, Cox, wouldn't pass the baton until he dropped dead. However, after my dad stepped down, the prez also decided to retire. He lived on a farm less than a half hour from the club, and at first, I thought he'd be all up in Fox's business, but Cox was content to let Fox and I do our thing.

We worked well together, but that didn't mean we always saw eye to eye. Like the last time I'd escorted a Silver Saint female to our compound.

"The fuck is wrong with you, Maverick?" Fox growled as soon as I shut his door and sat in a chair across from his desk. "Warned you the last time you snatched a Silver Saint old lady that we were gonna have a problem. Fucking hell, you're putting me in a shitty position."

"First, it bears repeating that I didn't know she belonged to them when I took Lorelei," I pointed out. "Second, Molly isn't an old lady." Yet.

"She's the oldest daughter of the fucking president!" Fox bellowed as he shoved back from his desk and shot to his feet. "The ultimate club princess." He started pacing, a dark scowl on his face as he continued. "She's un-fucking-touchable!"

Coming to a halt in front of me, he crossed his arms over his chest and stared down at me with an expression that would have had just about any other man crying for their momma. "Take her back. Now. Gonna try to get ahead of this and see if I can avoid war with the fucking Silver Saints."

I jumped up and got in his face, consumed with rage over his order. "Never gonna fucking happen, Fox," I seethed. "Molly is not going anywhere." In any other time and circumstance, I would not go against Fox. He was a president and my best friend, and I respected those roles. But when it came to my woman, there was no boundary I wouldn't cross. Nothing I wouldn't do to keep her.

"Paper-thin fucking ice, Maverick." His chest

expanded slowly as he sucked in a deep breath, then exhaled it evenly. A muscle jumped in his jaw, and he took a single step closer, bringing us less than a foot apart. "Last time you put us in the Silver Saints' crosshairs, your sister's connection saved you and gave me an excuse not to kick your ass to the curb. You don't have that ace up your sleeve this time."

"I—"

Fox held up his hand so I swallowed what I was going to say and waited until he was ready to hear it.

"You've been my brother since the day you were born. Always trusted you, and while it got a little dented in the situation with Kansas, it didn't break. So I'm gonna give you one shot to convince me why I shouldn't kick your ass and dump you on the street with the garbage, then take Molly back myself. One chance to convince me that I should back you on this."

"She's mine." The truth was the only defense I had. "Moment I met her, I knew. Soon as I can convince her of that, I'll get my property patch on her and my baby in her belly."

Fox's eyes widened ever so slightly, I'd have missed it if I didn't know him so well. "You're sure you can convince her to agree?"

I nodded.

"Willing to bet the club on it? Because that's what you're doing. If I let her stay even a few more hours, I'm making it clear that we are behind you." Fox pressed his lips together and narrowed his eyes, studying me intently.

When I didn't flinch, or even react, some of the tension in his shoulders leached out, and I let out a mental sigh of relief. "She's it for me, brother," I told him. "Need to call Tank and have his old lady work on a property patch."

Fox nodded and dropped his arms as he made his way back around his desk and sat. "He's here for a meeting. I'll let him know."

We talked business for a few minutes, but I was anxious to get back to my girl.

"Go. Figure your shit out. You still good to hold down the fort tomorrow?"

We had a run scheduled, and Fox liked to go from time to time, so I'd run shit while he was gone. Plus, this was a contact who would only work with me or Fox, so one of us had to go.

"Yeah." I stood and jerked my chin up at him in farewell before starting for the door.

"Mav."

I was at the threshold when I heard him say my name, so I halted and turned around.

"Better get her on board real fucking fast. She's the only person who'll be able to save your ass from a man the Devil himself wouldn't cross."

4

MOLLY

Cooling my jets in Maverick's room while he had it out with his president wasn't my idea of a good time, but I distracted myself by being nosy. He was only gone for about half an hour, but it was long enough for me to go through his medicine cabinet, under the bathroom sink, his dresser and bedside table drawers, and glance in his closet.

Most people probably called what I was doing an invasion of his privacy, but he'd left me alone in his space after basically kidnapping me, so I figured that all bets were off. And I was curious about the guy who had brought my nonexistent libido to life. Plus, I'd learned from my dad how important gathering intel was. If they wouldn't have gone running straight to him, I would've asked Hack or Grey to look into Maverick for me after the big birthday party at the compound.

Since I didn't have any hacking skills of my own, I had to settle for snooping around while I had the chance. Not that I learned much other than the man was a neat freak who only wore jeans, leather, and T-shirts and wasn't big on personal mementos. There wasn't a single photo in his room, and all of the flat surfaces were bare.

I didn't want to get caught red-handed, so when I heard the beeping of the security panel on the door, I raced over to the oversized chair in the corner. Just as I dropped onto it, Maverick came into the room.

His gaze zeroed in on me, and he kicked the door shut behind him. "Sorry I had to leave you like that, princess."

Shifting in my seat to get a little more comfortable, I shrugged. "I know how it is. When the prez wants to have a chat, you're gonna talk. Doesn't matter if you're the VP or the timing is bad."

"It's a bonus for me, you being used to club life." Settling on the edge of the bed directly across from me, he rested his elbows on his thighs as he smiled at me. "And that you were willing to be kidnapped."

I shook my head with a soft laugh. "Only because it was you doing the kidnapping."

"Damn straight." His blue orbs burned into mine. "A man would have to be out of his mind to take you from the Silver Saints compound, and no other guy is ever gonna get close enough to you to ever even consider the possibility of taking you from here."

If he kept this up, my panties were going to spontaneously combust. But I couldn't let that happen until we had some things figured out. "As sexy as all this possessive talk is, you still haven't clued me into what any of this means to you."

"You gotta know that snatching you from Silver Ink could only mean one thing. I plan—"

My stomach chose that exact moment to let out a loud growl, pissing me off because it wasn't something Maverick was willing to ignore.

Getting to his feet, he held his hand out to me. "First, we fill your belly, then I'll satisfy your curiosity. For everything."

"Fine, dammit," I huffed, sliding my palm against his. "But you better have someone around here who knows how to cook because I might be amazing in the tattoo parlor, but I'm not so great in the kitchen."

"Can't say it'll be gourmet or any shit like that,

but Biscuit makes some damn good basic home cook-ing," he assured me as he led me downstairs, through the main room, around to the back of the bar, and through the door to the kitchen.

When a delicious scent hit my nose, I wasn't surprised to find a group of guys lined up at one of the long tables since the Silver Saints hung out in the kitchen whenever there was food that someone else had cooked available. The only one I recognized was Fox, who was seated at the head of the table. He was also the only man who didn't look surprised to see me at Maverick's side.

The guy next to Fox got to his feet and shook his head. I recognized the road name on his cut, Blade. He was the Iron Rogues doctor like Patch was for the Silver Saints.

"Shit, Maverick." He grabbed his empty plate off the table and walked it over to the sink. "Thought Pike was fucking around when he said you brought a woman to the clubhouse."

"Never a damn joke when our VP kidnaps a woman who belongs to the Silver Saints," Fox grum-bled before digging into the spaghetti piled on the plate in front of him.

Several heads jerked back, eyes going wide with shock. The man who'd been sitting on the other side of Blade heaved a deep sigh. The patches on his cut let me know he was the Iron Rogues Treasurer, Phoenix. "Shit, man. I do my best to fill our coffers till they're overflowing, but we could have all the money in the world, and it wouldn't do us a damn bit of good if you piss off the Silver Saints by taking another one of their old ladies."

"Do you see a property patch on me?" I asked, pointing at my tank. "I'm nobody's old lady."

"Holy fuck. She's one of Mac's daughters, isn't she?" the guy at the far end of the table groaned. "That's even worse. He does not play when it comes to his girls. Not even a fucking tiny bit."

"Calm your tits, Viper." Maverick guided me over to where a pot of sauce, a bowl of thin spaghetti noodles, and a platter of garlic bread were lined up next to a stack of plates. "There's not gonna be any blowback against the club. Molly is here of her own free will."

Viper shook his head. "As if that's gonna be good enough for the Silver Saints prez."

Scooping some pasta onto a plate, I winked at Maverick and added, "I'm not sure that I'd call it my own free will when you carried me out over your shoulder."

"We both know you wouldn't have ridden all the

way here if you weren't more than okay with me taking you," Maverick chided as he spooned sauce over my noodles. Then he dropped a piece of garlic bread next to it before making his own plate.

Once that was done, he led me to the side of the table where none of his club brothers sat. After he settled me into a seat the farthest away from them, he sat down and wrapped his arm around the back of my chair.

I was lifting my fork to my mouth when I noticed Fox was focused on me. When our gazes met, he asked, "Is Maverick right?"

Although the president of the Iron Rogues was an intimidating man, I'd grown up surrounded by guys who were just like him. It would take a lot more than his glare to scare me. "About what?"

Maverick shook his head with a deep chuckle, shoving some spaghetti into his mouth instead of interfering.

"About your dad not blaming my whole fucking club for the stunt Mav pulled, carrying you out of Silver Ink," Fox replied.

Leaning into Maverick's side, I grinned at Fox. "My dad might think he's the boss of me, but he's not. I'm twenty-five years old. If I want to let a man carry me out to his bike and go for a ride over state lines with him, I can."

"Pretty fucking sure that logic won't stop your dad from putting my VP six feet under for daring to come near you," Fox disagreed.

"Over state fucking lines," Phoenix echoed my words with a deep sigh. "Gonna have to make sure I have bail money if there are federal charges, assuming Maverick isn't dead."

I hummed as I finally took my first bite of spaghetti, the flavors exploding on my tongue. "Mmm, yum."

The only guy who hadn't spoken yet lifted his chin toward me. "Glad you like it."

He wore a white apron with red splotches on it, so I couldn't read the name stitched on the front of his cut. But it was easy to guess who he was. "Thanks for cooking, Biscuit. It tastes delicious."

"You're welcome," he muttered before finishing the rest of his meal and getting up.

I listened to the banter between the men while I polished off my spaghetti, wondering what Fox meant when he said, "Remember what I said, Maverick. Get it done soon."

Assuming it was club business, I didn't ask. Instead, I focused on finishing my meal. Once I finished and Maverick rinsed off our plates, I gripped his arm. "Okay, you've stalled long enough. Why did you bring me here?"

Viper nodded. "Yeah, we're all dying to know."

Maverick glared at his club brother and tossed me over his shoulder. Again. And it was just as sexy this time around.

5

MAVERICK

I bit back a laugh at Molly's outraged gasp when I gave her ass a little slap while marching out of the kitchen with her over my shoulder.

"Is this going to become a thing?" she huffed. "You can't just toss me over your shoulder whenever you aren't getting your way."

"Wanna bet?"

"Sure. If I win, you have to be honest with me about why you brought me here."

I stopped outside my room and quickly unlocked it, then entered, shut the door, and twisted the lock before setting her back on her feet.

"I have no problem being honest, princess. As long as you do the same."

Molly frowned and looked up at me as she

planted her hands on her hips, causing her tits to thrust out. I swallowed hard, trying not to drool over the mouthwatering sight. I couldn't wait to have those in my hands, in my mouth, around my cock...*Fuck. Head in the damn game, Mav.*

"When have I ever been dishonest with you?"

I took her hand and led her over to the couch, where I took a seat, then grasped her hips and picked her up, settling her on my lap so she strad-dled my legs. "We both know why I took you, princess," I muttered softly as I pulled on the elastic holding all her gorgeous curls on top of her head. "If you're gonna keep pretending you don't, then you're lying."

Molly's lips formed a cute little pout for a moment—until she realized what she was doing and flattened them into a line. "Maybe I don't want to assume."

I mulled that over for a second, then nodded. "That's fair. Okay. I'll make it real clear." My hands palmed her ass, and I scooted her forward so the bulge in my jeans was snuggled into the apex of her thighs. "I want you. From the moment I saw you, I knew I had to have you." I put my hand over her mouth when she opened it and raised an eyebrow. "And before you say it, no, I don't just want to fuck you—although that is definitely high on my priority list."

She nipped at my fingers, and I took my hand away before grabbing her butt and yanking her even tighter against me, smirking when she shivered. "You're playing with fire, baby."

"If you don't just want to...to..."

"Fuck you?" I supplied, loving that this sexy, confident creature was suddenly blushing. It was adorable as hell. "Molly, the first time I saw you, you'd just been knocked on your ass by a bunch of little kids. Felt like I'd been knocked down with you. Because yeah, the first thing I wanted to do was fuck you, but that wasn't only because you're the sexiest woman I've ever seen. I wanted to put one of those cute little monsters of my own right here." I splayed one of my hands over her stomach and winked when her eyes grew wide as saucers. A smug grin stole over my lips at the desire simmering in her green pools.

"I wanted to claim you in every way possible. You know we don't use that term lightly, princess."

She'd grown up in the life, so she knew exactly how serious I was when I used that word.

"You can't just decide to claim me, Maverick," Molly huffed. "Don't you think I should have a say in whether I want you to claim me?"

"You already did, baby," I practically purred as I bent my head and ran the tip of my nose up her jaw, inhaling her delicious scent. The position pressed her tits into my chest, and her hard nipples poked through her shirt.

"What?"

"Your body knows who it belongs to, princess. If your brain needs a little more convincing, I'm more than happy to help you out."

I moved down to her throat and licked over her fluttering pulse, then I took my hand from her stomach and hooked a finger around the top edge of her tank and bra. Dragging it down, I licked my lips as I exposed her left breast. It was full and round, dotted with sexy little freckles. My tongue flicked the hard tip before I blew on it, and Molly moaned as she squirmed on my lap.

"Need more proof?" I mumbled as I closed my mouth around the rigid bud.

Her hands tunneled into my hair, and she moaned while arching her back.

My cock was...oversized...so even though my girl was tiny, my painfully hard shaft was rubbing against Molly's hot pussy every time she moved. I wasn't going to be able to tease much longer without losing it.

After giving her breast plenty of attention, I freed the other and... *Holy fucking shit.*

I blinked, unsure if what I saw was real. It was. Molly's nipple had a tiny silver hoop pierced through it.

"Damn, princess," I rasped, my throat tight with the effort not to come just looking at her. "Your tits are spectacular, but...fuck..."

"You like it?"

My gaze whipped up to her face when I heard the hesitant note in her voice. She watched me nervously.

"Baby, that is the sexiest thing I have ever seen. Please tell me your sister did this so I don't lose my shit."

She giggled and nodded, making me sigh with relief.

I leaned in and licked her decorated tip, leaking come when she gasped, grinding herself down on my painfully hard dick. When I tugged the little ring between my teeth, she grasped my biceps, digging her nails into my flesh as she cried out.

I wanted to spend more time focused on her tits, but if I didn't get inside her soon, I was gonna blow in my pants like a fucking teenager. I let her nipple go and raised my head, staring at her lust-glazed eyes, her mouth pink and swollen from biting back her moans. That thought pissed me off. Not only didn't I want her keeping her sounds from me, but I was the only one allowed to bite those plump lips.

My hands slid up to cradle her face, and I swallowed hard in anticipation before I finally gave myself permission to kiss her without restraint. I nipped the corner of her lips, and she gasped, giving me the opening I wanted. Sweeping my tongue inside, I groaned at the burst of flavor. She tasted like sunshine and strawberries.

My hands cupped her perfect tits, my fingers rolling and plucking the tips. She moaned and squirmed on my lap while tangling her tongue with mine, desperately kissing me back as though she had no other choice.

I broke away just so I could pull her top off, then unhooked her bra and toss it away.

"Maverick," Molly whimpered, watching me with hooded eyes. She slipped her hands under my shirt and glided them up my chest as she leaned in to trace her tongue along the design on my neck.

"Fuck, Molly. I need to be in you," I grunted, shoving to my feet and stalking to the bed.

She shivered and whispered, "Yes, please."

I laid her on the mattress and shrugged my cut

off my shoulders before whipping my T-shirt over my head. Then I bent over her and pulled down her leather leggings and underwear at the same time.

Fuck, she was amazing. Creamy skin covered in mouthwatering freckles, big tits, and sweetly curved hips. I paused my perusal of her body when my gaze landed on her flat stomach. The desire to fill her with my come until she was round with my baby rode me hard.

"You are so fucking gorgeous, baby," I breathed as I shucked my jeans and crawled onto the bed.

"Um...Mav?"

"Yeah, princess?" I looked at her expression and immediately stopped at the fear I saw there.

"You are...um...I don't think that thing...it's really big and..."

I chuckled when I realized what she was stammering about, earning myself a cute little glare. She squeezed her legs together, and I ran a soothing palm up her thigh to lightly cup her pussy. "I know you're small, but we'll go slow. You'll take every inch of me, Molly. This pussy was made for me."

"But—"

"You trust me?"

"Yes," she replied without hesitation.

I smiled gently and placed a kiss just above her pubic bone. "Trust me to make it good for you."

"I do, it's just that, um…I haven't…"

Her cheeks bloomed with color, and my heartbeat accelerated as I thought about what she was trying to tell me.

"Are you a virgin, baby?"

Molly nodded. "I've been waiting for…I want what my parents have. Besides, no guy has ever been willing to stand up to my dad."

"Fuck," I growled as I surged up to capture her mouth in a soul-deep kiss.

When we broke apart, gasping for air, she panted, "You're okay with that?"

"Are you fucking kidding me?" I planted my fists on either side of her body so I could hover above her. "There is nothing that would keep me from wanting you, baby. But knowing you're untouched…fuck. Mine. Only mine." I kissed her again, then watched her beautiful face as I slid down her body and opened her legs so I could kneel between them.

Finally, I dropped my eyes to her center and used my hands on her thighs to push her legs as far apart as possible. My breath caught in my throat when something glinted between the folds of her pussy. Slowly, I used my thumbs to part her southern lips, and when I spotted the bejeweled barbell pierced through the hood of her clit, I was hit with a rush of desire so strong it made my head spin. My mouth watered, and I felt something primal rip to the surface, taking over as I fell onto my stomach.

Her pussy was pink and swollen, slick with arousal, and it made the piece of jewelry shine, as if it was begging for attention. "So fucking perfect," I groaned before lowering my head and inhaling deeply. Sunshine and strawberries.

I licked up her center, then gently tugged on the little barbell.

"Maverick!" Molly gasped, her hips bucking wildly. Her hands moved to the top of my head and clenched my hair, causing my scalp to sting and turning me on even more.

She was so damn responsive, it pushed me to drive her out of control. I wanted to see her lost to the passion between us, writhing from the pleasure only I could give her, screaming my name as she fell apart.

I ate her like she was my last meal, drinking down her juices and playing with her pretty little clit. When she shook with need and begged for relief, I worked two fingers into her channel, then curled them up to scrape her G-spot as I sucked on her clit. Her back arched right before she shattered, screaming my name.

Mesmerized, I stared at her in wonder while I used my mouth and fingers to work her through her orgasm. Only when she was slumped on the bed, trembling and panting, did I finally move to cover her body with my own.

My cock bumped her clit, and she cried out, clutching the sheets in her fists at her sides.

"Are you on birth control, Molly?" I wasn't sure if I wanted her answer to be yes or no. I shouldn't take her bare if she wasn't...but the part of me that wanted to knock her up was overruling the rest.

She blinked, trying to clear away some of the haziness as she thought about my question. "No. Do you have protection?"

I shook my head. "Even if I did, I don't think I could use it with you, princess. I need to feel your pussy squeezing the fuck out of my bare cock. I haven't been with a woman in"—I thought about it for a second, then shook my head—"damn, I can't remember how long."

My dick nudged her opening again, and I bent my head, running my nose up her jaw until I reached her ear. "Don't want anything between us, baby." I didn't wait for her to respond before slowly pushing the fat head of my cock inside her.

"Shit. You're so fucking tight," I groaned. She was wrapped around me like a vise, making it hard to concentrate on being gentle. I hooked my arms under her knees and raised them up to change the angle so I slid in a little easier. Luckily, she was fucking drenched. I made the mistake of looking down at where we were joined, and seeing my dick disappearing into her sex sent a shaft of need slicing through me. Before I could control myself, I plunged deep, sinking in until I bottomed out, and my tip bumped against her cervix.

Molly cried out, and I froze.

"Son of a bitch!" My eyes flew to her face, and the pain I saw there made me frantically try to decide whether it would be better to pull out or stay still while she adjusted to my invasion. Molly was so tiny compared to me. I couldn't help being proud that she'd taken me all the way on the first thrust. "Are you okay?"

My jaw was clenched so hard from trying not to move that I was surprised it didn't break. But I was gentle as I wiped away the tears leaking from her beautiful green eyes.

"It-it hurt, but...I think...I need..."

"What, baby?"

"Can you, I think I need you to move."

"Like this?" I gritted my teeth and slowly inched back, then carefully pushed back in.

"Yesss," she moaned, her inner muscles clenching. "But more."

I eased out of her almost all the way before thrusting home once more.

"Oh, yes! Maverick!" she shouted, breaking the last of my control.

Pulling out to the tip again, I slammed back inside. "Fuck!" I knew I should be gentle, but the beast inside me had taken over, and I couldn't stop. My hips pistoned in and out, fighting to leave her tight channel as she clamped down hard. "That's it, princess," I grunted. "Fight me. Your greedy pussy doesn't want to let me go."

"Maverick," she whined, digging her nails into my arms. "Oh, yes! Yes!"

"You're mine, Molly. Gonna live inside this pussy. Fill you full with my come and put my baby in you."

I hadn't even realized I said those words out loud until she gasped and froze for a beat. Her body had no hesitation, though. Her legs circled my waist, and her inner muscles tightened, massaging my dick and milking my orgasm from me.

Slipping a hand between us, I flicked her clit piercing, which sent her into a spiral until she detonated around my shaft.

I fucked her hard and deep, determined to claim her inside and out. "Fuck, baby. Oh, fuck yeah. That's it, Molly. Squeeze that pussy. Fuck!"

Two more thrusts and my orgasm barreled into me like a fucking freight train. As my jizz exploded from my cock, I threw my head back and bellowed, "MINE!"

6

MOLLY

Until he showed up at Silver Ink yesterday morning, waking up wrapped in Maverick's arms wasn't something I expected to ever happen. I knew he felt the attraction between us when we first met, but I didn't think he would act on it because he didn't want any trouble with my dad. No one had ever been brave enough to fight for me.

I couldn't picture any of the Silver Saints waiting two weeks to make a move on the woman they wanted, so not hearing anything from him for that long had crushed any hope I'd had. But it all came rushing back when I realized he'd made an appointment for me to ink him—something I fully intended to do at some point.

Shifting in his hold, I traced my finger over the

black ink on the arm around my waist. When he brushed his lips against my temple, I tilted my head back to look up at him. "I want to put my mark on you."

"Every bare inch of my skin is yours. Put your ink all over me, princess," he murmured.

I could tell from the quality of the artwork that his tattoos were important to him, which made the offer even more special. "I'd love that. Thank you."

"Just tell me when and which spot you want to start with."

I grinned up at him. "You have something specific in mind?"

"Nope." His scruff scraped against my shoulder as he pressed a kiss to the pulse point at the base of my neck. "Artist's choice for the first one."

"Really?" It was a rare thing for someone to trust me to ink them without any input on the design. So much so that Dahlia was the only person who'd gone in blind, back when I was first learning.

"Yup, you're talented as shit." He curled his arm to turn me so that I was sprawled against his chest. "And I trust you not to fuck me over with the design."

Grinning down at him, I traced my finger over a

blank spot of skin on his shoulder. "So you don't want a No Regerts tattoo right here?"

"Keep it up, and you're gonna earn yourself a spanking." He shook his head with a deep chuckle, lightly swatting my butt.

I wiggled on top of him, pressing my thighs together at the tingle his words evoked. "Don't threaten me with a good time."

"It'd be one that'd leave you feeling the imprint of my hand for a few days." His phone chirped with a text notification just as my inner walls clenched at his warning. "Hold that thought, princess."

Reaching out to pluck his cell off the nightstand, he glanced at the screen with a groan.

"You gotta go?" I asked with a sigh.

"Yup, but hopefully it won't be long."

He claimed my mouth in a deep kiss that left me breathless. Then he climbed off the mattress and threw on some clothes. When he left the room, I grabbed my phone to call my sister.

Dahlia picked up in the middle of the first ring. "Took you long enough to check in. I was starting to think maybe it was wrong of me not to clue Dad in on what happened yesterday."

"It's only been a day, which is exactly what I promised," I pointed out.

"Yeah, but you know I've been dying of curiosity." She made a tsk-ing sound. "It's not every day that my sister is hauled over the shoulder of the Iron Rogues' VP and rides off on the back of his bike to who knows where."

Curling up against his pillow, I pulled the sheet higher. "He brought me to their territory."

"Damn," she breathed. "I should've guessed that since he looked pretty damn serious when he carried you out of Silver Ink."

"And I gave him my V-card last night," I confessed.

"Am I supposed to be surprised?" Dahlia snorted. "Because I'm not. The chemistry between the two of you was hot enough to set the tattoo parlor on fire."

I hadn't planned on telling her the most important part of what happened last night, but I found myself blurting, "We didn't use a condom, and you already know I'm not on birth control since there was no need before I met Maverick and I didn't think I'd ever see him again."

"You know what that means, right?"

Resting my hand over my lower belly, I answered, "That I could be pregnant?"

"Well, that too, but also that this thing between

the two of you isn't temporary. It's gotta be permanent if he's trying to knock you up on day one." She whistled the tune to a lullaby our mom used to sing to each of us kids when we were babies. "We've seen it time and time again when one of the guys falls hard and fast. They always want to knock our aunts up. It's like the biker mating dance, literally and figuratively. That's why there's so many children running around the compound."

"Do you think so?" Maverick and I hadn't really talked about the lack of protection last night, except for the dirty, hot things he'd said while he was inside me.

"Yup, which is why I hate to burst your bubble. But Dad has already noticed you're not around," she told me.

"Crap," I groaned, burying my face in a pillow to muffle my scream of frustration.

"I called your appointments for the next few days to let them know they needed to reschedule, but one of them missed the message and came into Silver Ink first thing this morning anyway," she explained. "Patriot was there and did his session, so no worries about the client. But then he wanted to know why you weren't around, and I told him you were helping a friend who had some stuff going on."

I buried my face in the pillow again with a groan.

"Yeah, that went over how you'd expect."

Rolling onto my back, I murmured, "Like a lead balloon since pretty much all of my friends are connected to the club."

"Yup, but I said it was a girl we went to school with who you hadn't talked to in a while but was cool even though she didn't have many friends." I was about to thank my sister for her quick thinking when she added, "He backed off, but he must've called Dad as soon as the appointment was done because he popped in like five minutes after the client left."

"Crap."

"So you'd better send Mom a text or something so she can keep Dad off your back, at least for a few more days," she suggested.

"Will do. Sorry you had to lie to Dad for me."

"I'm sure you'll have to do the same for me some-day," she said with a laugh. "Besides, Dad is lucky we didn't rebel harder, considering how overprotective he is."

"True."

We chatted for a little longer, and then when we hung up, I fired off a quick message to my mom, letting her know that I was fine and to talk my dad off the ledge if he couldn't handle not knowing where I was. Then I raided Maverick's dresser for a pair of sweatpants and a T-shirt. Just when I finished with a shower and was dressed, he came stomping back into the room.

"What's wrong?"

"Fuck." He raked his fingers through his hair. "I gotta go for a bit. Fox has to leave on a run, so I have to deal with some shit."

His explanation was vague, but I knew better than to ask any questions about club business. "Don't worry. I know you wouldn't leave right now if you didn't have to."

"My princess is so fucking perfect," he murmured before giving me a deep kiss.

When he finally lifted his head, I nudged him toward his closet. "The sooner you leave, the sooner you'll be back."

While Maverick was showering, my cell dinged. Glancing down at the screen, I smiled.

MOM

Don't worry, sweetie. I'll tell him it's girl stuff, and you're still in touch with me, so you're good. That should hold him off for at least an hour. LOL

It'd better be longer than that...or else Maverick

and I were screwed. We needed time to figure out what happened next. I frowned as I thought about what I'd do when Mav was doing club business or out on a run. I was going to be stuck twiddling my thumbs with nothing to do.

Maverick pulled on a pair of black jeans and a black T-shirt, then strode over to me. "What's wrong?"

"It's just," I heaved a deep sigh. "What am I supposed to do while you're busy? I'm not the kind of person who can sit around all day."

Wrapping his hand around my arm, he pulled me to my feet. "I can't do shit about having shit to do for Fox, but I can fix this."

7

MAVERICK

I held up my vest for Molly to stick her arms into, and when she did so without hesitation, I brought her close for a deep kiss. When I pulled back, I couldn't help grinning smugly at the dazed expression on her beautiful face. I wanted to take her back to bed and turn the simmer in her green pools into an inferno. To kiss every inch of her skin, lick every adorable freckle, and spend a fuck of a lot more time playing with her sexy as fuck piercings. But I had shit to do before I could take her back to bed.

Taking her hand, I walked with her through the clubhouse and out the front gate onto the street. Iron Inkworks was only two blocks away, so we were there in a few minutes.

I held the door open, and she stepped inside,

then stopped and breathed, "Whoa." Her eyes scanned all around, taking everything in, and even though I'd had nothing to do with the business, I couldn't help feeling proud at her awed reaction. Mostly though, I was relieved, because if she'd hated it, it would have made shit much harder.

The style was industrial, with concrete walls and floor, exposed beams, pipes, ductwork, and even metal grates separating the workstations. It would have been very stark and bleak if not for the rich, brown leather furniture, sepia-toned photographs on the walls, and other touches like a vintage jukebox, potted plants, and an old wood-burning stove "fireplace" in the waiting area.

"The vibe here is awesome," Molly murmured.

"Maverick."

I tore my gaze away from Molly to meet Whiskey's light brown eyes as he walked toward us with a scowl on his face—basically his permanent expression. Whiskey was our sergeant at arms, managed Iron Inkworks, and was an unbelievably talented artist. He wore his cut with a white T-shirt underneath that showcased his full sleeves on each arm, going all the way down to his fingers. His neck was also covered in ink, a design very similar to mine. We'd served in the military together, and the tats had meaning only to us.

"Whiskey," I said with a lift of my chin. "This is my woman, Molly."

Whiskey's brows rose, and his eyes dropped to my girl, then back up to me. "Yours?"

"Mine," I confirmed, tucking her into my side. "Know you're always looking for good talent. So I brought her to meet you."

"I am," he drawled, scratching the dark scruff on his chin. "How much experience does she have?"

"*She* is right here and can speak for herself," Molly snapped.

Whiskey wasn't trying to be an asshole just for the sake of being one. He was taking stock of her strength and thick skin. He wasn't aware of her background and wanted to make sure she could hold her own around a bunch of bikers.

I grinned but didn't say anything because she could run circles around him if she wanted to.

"Well?" he grouched when she didn't continue. "I don't have all fucking day."

Molly blinked and replied in a too sweet voice, "I'm sorry, did you ask me a question?"

One corner of Whiskey's mouth twitched—the most I'd ever seen him smile. "Experience?"

She popped a hip out and put her hand on it, looking up at him with a haughty expression. I wasn't sure what it said about me that I found it so damn hot. Then again, everything Molly did make me want to drag her to the nearest flat surface and fuck her.

"Why don't I just show you my portfolio?" She held out her arm and flipped it up to show off an intricately colored butterfly on her forearm. Then she bent over and shoved up her pant leg to reveal another design that was more incredible than the first. After that, she grabbed the hem of her shirt and started to raise it.

Before she could show more than a glimpse of her skin, I growled and put my arms around her from behind, yanking the sides of my vest closed. "That's enough proof," I muttered. "Molly is incredible, and you'd be lucky as fuck to have her working here."

Whiskey rolled his eyes and motioned for us to follow, then turned and headed back into the shop, stopping when he reached the first empty station. "I agree that you're very talented," he grumbled Molly as he crossed his large arms over his broad chest.

My lips tipped up again when Molly didn't even

glance at him before prowling around the small area and inspecting everything.

He watched her with a critical eye, observing how she handled the equipment and gauging her familiarity with it. "We have a new client in ten minutes. You can do his ink. Show me what you've got."

I frowned at my brother, my eyes arrowed in warning. "No."

Molly whirled around and glared at me. "What do you mean, no? We agreed—"

"I agreed to let you work here," I stated firmly.

Whiskey grunted. "Relax, Mav. The tat is on his fucking shoulder."

It was on the tip of my tongue to argue, but Molly's stance deflated a little, and I knew I'd have to give in. As much as I hated her being so close to other men—especially when they weren't someone I knew I could trust—I wanted her to be happy. "Fine," I gritted through clenched teeth. Her beaming smile made it worth it, but I still had conditions. "I'm not going to pretend the thought of you being so close to other men doesn't make me want to fucking kill someone, but as long as no clothes need to be removed, I'll keep my finger off my trigger."

Molly cocked her head to the side and studied me for a moment, and then she sighed. "Deal."

I reached out and captured her wrist, tugging her into my body, then put one hand on her hip and the other cradling the back of her head. "If I see one asshole trying to touch what's mine..." I growled.

"I'll break their wrist," she informed me haughtily.

Laughter burst from my chest before I sealed my mouth over hers. Fuck, I loved this woman. Feisty and sweet all rolled into one.

My tongue slipped into her mouth, and the hand on her hip slid down to her ass. Molly moaned and melted into my arms, giving as good as she got. I deepened the kiss, determined to make sure she wouldn't forget who the fuck she belonged to while I was out doing shit.

I was seconds away from dragging her to the nearest room with a door when the clearing of a throat broke through our passionate haze.

"Take it back to your room, Mav," Whiskey grunted. "Actually, let her breathe and move your ass because her client will be here any minute."

Reluctantly, I eased off the kiss, giving Molly a cocky smile when she clung to me as if she needed help staying upright. I fucking loved that she was so responsive and as affected by me as I was by her.

After a minute, she inhaled deeply and took a step back. Looking up at me, she shook her head. "Stop looking so smug."

Before I could reply, the door opened, and Fox stomped in, calling my name. He jerked his head toward the office, and I nodded. "Hold tight, princess," I told Molly with a quick, hard kiss to her lips. Then I followed Fox into the other room, shutting the door behind me.

"Shit went sideways at the port," Fox muttered without any preamble. "The shipping containers were mislabeled, and it's gonna take a day for our contacts to sort it. Since he's not on this run, I sent Storm to handle shit there."

Storm was our road captain and coordinated all of our runs, but he also led most of them because it satisfied his wanderlust. He was also an expert negotiator.

I nodded, crossing my arms over my chest and leaning back against the wall. "He'll get it done. I'll get on the phone with Cordell and let him know that it will be a partial delivery. Stone can take the rest up when—"

Fox held up his hand, cutting me off. "Cordell

already called me, pissed as fuck. He's paranoid and demanded I be the one to escort the final shipment."

"Then I can go to the port, and Storm can go on this run."

Prez shook his head and sighed, sitting on the desk behind him. "You know what I'm going to say, Mav."

"No." I wasn't going to let that bastard drag me away from my woman the day after I brought her home. While shit was still unsettled with Mac.

"You know we'll protect her."

I trusted my brothers with my life, but things with Molly weren't that simple. I'd never be able to be truly secure in her safety unless I was the one there to watch over her. "And if her dad figures out what happened and loses his shit?"

He ran his hands through his short hair and exhaled harshly. "I'll deal with Mac. Just get on the road and get back fast."

"Cordell and I are gonna have words about this bullshit, Fox. I'm tired of his bullshit. You know he only demands to work with you or me because it makes him look as though he's in control of the situation?"

"Showing off for the rest of the family by only dealing with the top of the food chain. I'm aware,"

Fox said dryly. He sat for a few beats, clearly thinking through something, then he stood and nodded. "Fine. Try not to lose him as a client but make it clear that he doesn't call the shots anymore. He doesn't agree, we'll cut him loose."

"Done." I pushed away from the wall and yanked open the door. Once I stepped over the threshold, my eyes immediately sought out my gorgeous redhead. A man around my age was sitting in her chair, and they were talking quietly. He was dressed in jeans, a T-shirt, a leather vest, and leather cuffs on both wrists.

I rolled my eyes because there wasn't a wrinkle, stain, or any sign of wear on anything. The poser was trying to look badass since he was in a shop run by an MC. But his three-hundred-dollar haircut and manicured hands more than gave him away.

Molly was sketching and hadn't looked up at him once, which made me feel a little less homicidal when I noticed him checking her out. I stalked over and pulled her to her feet, then grasped her ass and hoisted her up so she had no choice but to circle my hips with her legs.

"What...?" she asked...clearly confused at what was happening.

"Kiss me," I demanded in a low growl.

"Maverick, I have a client," she hissed. "I'm working."

"Kiss. Me." My tone brooked no argument, and having grown up in my world, she knew that if she didn't do as she'd been told, I'd lose credibility.

She glared at me for half a second, then wound her arms around my neck and brushed her mouth lightly over mine.

"That is not how you kiss your man, baby." I didn't just kiss her, I possessed her mouth, claimed it, forced her to submit, acknowledging that she was mine. My cock was rock hard, and I couldn't help rubbing her against it as I devoured her. She moaned and tightened her arms around me.

Being with Molly was intoxicating, and I almost forgot where the fuck we were, and that we weren't alone. But as much as I'd needed this to tide me over while I was gone, I'd also needed to stake my claim.

"What was that about?" she asked breathlessly when I finally let her up for air.

"Who do you belong to, Molly?"

Her eyes narrowed, and she pressed her lips together, clearly irritated as she realized what I'd been doing.

"Molly," I snarled. "Who do you belong to?"

After a few breaths, she huffed and admitted, "You."

"Damn fucking right. I gotta go on a run, baby. Should be back in a few days," I told her. The spark of disappointment in her green pools soothed some of my raging possessiveness. "Fox was supposed to be the one going, but something came up that takes priority. The people involved will only deal with him or me, so I can't send anyone else instead. Fucking hate leaving you."

Molly sighed. "I know. I'll just keep myself busy until you get back."

I took her chin between my thumb and forefinger. "Wear my cut anytime you aren't in our room, do you understand?"

"Okay," she agreed. I slowly exhaled in relief that she didn't put up an argument.

"Be good." I kissed her again before setting her on her feet, then turned to go find Whiskey.

He was in the office Fox and I had just vacated, so I stepped inside and rapped my knuckles on the desk, drawing his attention from his computer.

"Shit with Cordell. Fox needs me to take over this run."

Whiskey's eyes darted behind me before meeting mine again, then he gave me a chin lift. It was his way of telling me he'd watch out for my girl, keep her safe.

Grunting my thanks, I stalked out of the office, snatched one more kiss from my woman, then left to get this shit over with.

_____

8

As much as I'd enjoyed slinging ink over the past week, I was beyond desperate for Maverick to get back. For a few different reasons.

Although we had only spent one day together, I missed him. Plus, my mom and Dahlia had both warned me just this morning that my time was running out with my dad. They could only hold him off for so long, and my call to him a couple of days ago had apparently left him suspicious instead of mollifying him. He'd said some crap about how my voice had sounded off.

Growing up with a father who didn't miss a thing was a pain in the butt, especially for my sisters and me since he was way overprotective when it came to us. He cut Dane a lot more slack, which was totally unfair. And probably a big part of why I didn't feel guilty about disappearing with Maverick. I should have at least the same freedom as my twenty-one-year-old brother. He was barely old enough to drink, but he was a fully patched in Silver Saint. If he took off with a woman, my dad would probably barely blink.

All thoughts of the double standard fled from my head when Whiskey tapped me on the shoulder and jerked his chin toward the door. "Let's go."

The Iron Rogue who ran their tattoo parlor was a man of few words, so I wasn't surprised by his abruptness. But I had no idea what he was talking about since I had a customer due soon. "Where?"

"Your man is a few minutes out." He flashed me a smile that looked more like a grimace. "Figured you'd want to see him right away."

I'd been sketching in a notebook that I tossed onto my station. "Hell yes, let's go."

"Scratcher will cover your appointment."

I had a ton of doubt about the club brother's skills when I first heard his road name, but it turned out to be ironic as hell. Scratcher had one of the steadiest hands I'd ever seen and a light touch with the ink. His art was impressive, too. "Cool, thanks."

He gestured toward the door again. "One of the prospects is on his way over to escort you."

I rolled my eyes with a huff. "It's two blocks in all Iron Rogue territory. I would've been fine on my own."

Whiskey crossed his arms over his chest and quirked a brow. "You know better than that. Your man would have my ass under normal circumstances, let alone with the shit that's been going on."

Ducking my head, I pressed my lips together as I thought about the third reason I'd been anxious for Maverick's return. "But—"

"Don't give me shit, Molly," he growled. "Not when you already owe me fucking huge for keeping my mouth shut."

It was hard to argue with logic like that. "You're right. Sorry."

Luckily, the prospect yanked the door open, ending our conversation before Whiskey could make me feel guilty over the fact that I had somehow managed to convince him to keep Maverick in the dark until he got back. I wasn't sure how dangerous the club business was, and I hadn't wanted to distract him. The fact that Whiskey agreed both relieved and worried me since it was a fairly safe bet that he wouldn't have if there hadn't been much risk on Maverick's run.

"Don't get so caught up in welcoming him back that you forget to loop him in. ASAP. I'm not gonna be too far behind you, and you don't want me to be the one to tell him."

"It'll be the first thing I do after giving him a big, wet kiss," I promised, heading for the door.

Whiskey shook his head with a groan, making the prospect chuckle. I giggled as I walked past Jake, then hurried down the sidewalk toward the clubhouse with him right next to me. I made the two-block walk in only a few minutes and arrived just as Maverick's bike turned through the gates. I raced after him and threw myself into his arms as soon as he climbed off his motorcycle.

"You're back," I cried.

"Fucking finally." He cupped my butt cheeks to lift me off the ground, so I wrapped my legs around his waist and twined my arms around his neck. "Missed you like hell, princess. Sorry I was gone so long."

"Missed you too," I whispered against his lips.

He gave me the kiss I'd been waiting for, his tongue sliding inside my mouth to tangle with mine until I was breathless with need. When he lifted his head, I let out a whimper of protest.

"Don't worry." He squeezed my butt. "I'm not going anywhere for a good long while. After the shit I just handled, Fox is gonna have to deal with the next fire that needs to be put out without my help. I plan on being buried deep in your pussy for the foreseeable future."

I beamed a smile up at him. "That plan sounds awesome to me, but we're going to need to come up for air sooner rather than later. Keeping my dad in the dark about where I am hasn't been easy. It's a good thing you came back today because I think our time has just about run out."

"We'll figure out the shit with your dad together, princess." He gave me another quick kiss. "I'm so fucking lucky you grew up in the life and aren't pissed I was gone longer than planned. I hate that you had to deal with putting your dad off while I wasn't here to help."

"It's okay," I reassured him. "My mom and sister pitched in to keep him distracted."

"It's a good thing your man is back," Jake called as he strode toward us with something clutched in his fist.

As he neared, I realized they were flowers. And

that I had run out of time to tell Maverick what had gone down while he was gone.

Maverick set me on my feet as he turned toward Jake. His eyes narrowed and a muscle jumped in his jaw as his gaze dropped to the flowers. "You bringing those to my woman, prospect?"

"Yeah, but it's not what you think." Jake tossed the flowers on the ground and held his hands up in a gesture of surrender. "They're not from me."

"Who the fuck are they from then?" Maverick growled as he leaned down to grab the bouquet off the ground.

"I wish I knew," Jake muttered. "If I figured that shit out, I'd get patched in for sure."

"You're a long way from being voted on." Maverick yanked the small white envelope out of the flowers, his brows drawing together as he read the note. "What the fuck?"

"If you're going to be angry with anyone, it should be me." I gripped his biceps to stop him from doing something he would regret—like throw a punch at the poor prospect who was in striking distance. Or go hunt down one of his club brothers for keeping this from him while he was gone. "I begged Whiskey to let you focus on club business while you were gone because I was scared you'd get hurt if you were distracted by this whole mess. And it's not like it's a huge deal or anything. Just some flowers and gifts from a random secret admirer."

"How many gifts, and when the fuck did this start?" Maverick snarled.

"Two bouquets of flowers, a box of chocolates, and a card," I rattled off with a sigh. "The roses were first and came to the tattoo shop the day after you left. The chocolates were a couple of days later. Then the card came to the clubhouse yesterday. Now these flowers."

"The guy switched from leaving you shit at Iron Inkworks to here, and my club still doesn't know who the fuck he is this many fucking days later?" Maverick growled.

I was worried for Whiskey's safety since he chose that moment to walk through the gates. But he didn't make it to us before he looked over his shoulder. My gaze followed...and I realized a bad situation had just gotten a hell of a lot worse.

9

MAVERICK

The roar of a motorcycle interrupted me before I could decide whether to put a bullet in Whiskey's or Jake's skull or just cut off their balls for not telling me about the "gifts" Molly had been receiving.

"What the fuck?"

Whiskey's exclamation drew my attention as he stalked toward the newcomer. I glanced over and cursed when I saw Cash Gannon—a fucking Silver Saint—climbing off his bike. He was holding an arm across his middle, and I could see blood darkening his gray T-shirt beneath his hand.

"Blade around?" he asked as if he just wanted to visit.

"Fucking hell," I muttered. As if shit wasn't

complicated enough finding out there was a motherfucker stalking my woman, now I had to deal with
this. I'd been banking on being able to handle the
"admirer" before shit went down with Mac and his
club. I pointed at one of the prospects hovering near
the entrance to the garage, smoking a cigarette. "Find
Blade. Tell him to bring his medical shit."

A female gasp made me grimace as I watched
Cash's gaze swing in Molly's direction.

"Are you okay?" she asked, rushing toward him. I
grabbed the belt loop of her jeans and hauled her
back against me. I could feel her glaring up at me,
but I didn't take my eyes off Cash.

"Molly?" Cash gaped. "What the fuck are
you...?" He trailed off when he spotted my arm
curling around her, keeping her in place. Then his
expression darkened and fury burned in his eyes.
"You're a fucking dead man, Maverick."

Molly startled at Cash's statement, and I knew
she was going to speak up, but that wasn't how this
world worked. Apparently, she needed a reminder
that her man would fight for her. I gave her a gentle
squeeze, and she huffed but stayed silent.

"You think I didn't know exactly what I was
risking when I brought Molly here?"

"You want a war?" Cash grunted, trying to

contain his shock.

"I want Molly."

He scoffed and shook his head. "Not a fucking chance in hell. And if you want a prayer of keeping a bullet out of your skull, she'll be leaving with me. Forget Blade," he ground out, clearly in pain but willing to leave anyway. "Molly, get on my bike."

I quickly maneuvered Molly behind me and took a threatening step forward. "She doesn't ride on anyone's bike but mine," I growled.

Cash scowled and snarled, "She's a Silver Saint princess, asshole. Molly, get on my fucking bike."

In a flash, I was in front of Cash with my hand around his throat. Normally, we would be pretty evenly matched, but not only was he injured, fury at the threat to my woman pumped heavy and hot through my veins. "She's an Iron Rogue old lady, motherfucker. She's *mine*."

Cash's free hand wrapped around my wrist, gripping it hard enough that I knew it would break if that was really his intention. Since I was aware of his restraint, I loosened my grip on his neck so he could speak. "I don't see a—"

"Property patch?" We both turned at the sound of Fox's voice. He stood beside Molly, who was slipping a black leather vest over her shoulders. Fox stood slightly in front of my woman and crossed his arms over his chest, his legs in a wide stance. "Look again."

Whiskey had moved to stand on Molly's other side, and he said something to her that only they could hear.

Her hair was already up on her head, so nothing was obscuring the back of her vest when she turned around.

Despite the situation, seeing "Property of Maverick" branding her caused my dick to harden. I wanted nothing more than to fuck her in that cut. *Only* the cut.

"Fucking hell," Cash grunted.

I released him and took several steps back. He was no longer a threat. I'd claimed Molly, and he had to respect that as long as she'd been willing. Since she'd put up no argument and was beaming at me when she turned around, there was nothing he could do.

Mac was a different situation altogether. I doubted he would give a fuck about my claim when it came to his daughter, and honestly...I respected him for it. I couldn't pretend that I would be any better with my daughters. Still, he'd have to come to terms with it eventually because the only way someone could take her away from me was if I was dead.

"Let me fix him up before you kick his ass, Maverick," Blade said with a sigh as he ambled over to us.

"Not gonna fight with you, Cash," I told the Silver Saint in a voice low enough that Molly wouldn't overhear. "And I'm not gonna stop you from telling Mac about us. But don't ever bring up taking her away from me again, or you'll be having a real close encounter with the end of my Glock."

Cash shook his head and let Blade lift his arm and drape it around his neck. "I think you're delusional about who will end up six feet under in this situation, Maverick."

I shrugged and watched them until they disappeared inside the clubhouse. Blade had a medical clinic set up in a building directly behind it.

Once they were gone, my eyes found my woman, and I purused her from head to toe, then back up again. I needed to fuck her. Licking my lips in anticipation, I prowled over, letting her see the dark hunger gnawing at me.

"How do I look?" she asked, her tone a little sassy, turning me on even more.

"Like you're mine," I grunted.

10

MOLLY

I knew there would be repercussions to Cash seeing me at the Iron Rogues clubhouse with Maverick, but I didn't want to think about my dad's reaction to my relationship right now. Or my secret admirer.

Instead, I wanted to celebrate the fact that I'd just become Maverick's old lady. And there was no better way to do that than by ourselves in our room.

Which he must've thought too because he tossed me over his shoulder yet again and carried me straight there. Then his lips were on mine, devouring me. I wanted nothing more than to feel them everywhere.

I leaned back, starting to slip off my property

vest, but he stopped his kisses, his eyes blazing as he hovered over me. "Keep that on, princess."

"You want me to keep my clothes on?" I balked, staring up at him through my lashes.

He grinned, tracing the lines of my cheek with his calloused fingers. "Not all of them. Just the vest. I want to see you wearing nothing but my property patch while you take my cock."

Fisting the front of my shirt, he pulled me closer to him, the thin lines of material ripping under his fingers as he pried away the fabric. Then he made quick work of my bra, and his smile broadened as he bent over, sucking my pierced nipple into his mouth.

I bucked forward, eager to feel more of him. My fingers tunneled through his thick auburn hair as I pressed my chest closer to his mouth and hissed, "Yes."

His free hand went to my other nipple, giving it the same twists as his tongue on my pierced one before his lips trailed down my breasts and to my stomach. His gaze was heated as he met mine before his tongue flickered just along the line of my jeans. "Are you drenched for me? Is this greedy little pussy ready for me to taste it?"

"Yes," I moaned, already bucking my hips forward.

He chuckled before yanking my pants down. "Such a greedy princess."

Normally, it would have taken me forever to get my boots and jeans off, but my man was eager and had my bare pussy up to his lips, my thighs over his shoulders in one fell swoop.

"I love this pussy," he murmured before he flattened his tongue against my folds.

"It loves your mouth right back, Maverick," I teased, pushing my hips forward.

"Such a greedy girl. My greedy girl," he whispered before spreading my legs and diving into my wet folds.

I thrust my hips so I could meet his tongue with my body. He laughed against my skin before sliding a finger against me, his lips toying with my clit piercing before sucking hard on my sensitive bundle of nerves.

My entire body was already on fire, and I was a woman possessed, bucking and gripping the sheets, chasing my orgasm. But just before I could feel the beautiful climax crest over me, Maverick abruptly stopped, popping off my pussy with a big wet grin.

"No, I was so close," I whimpered.

"I know, princess. But as much as I love to

devour your orgasms, I want to feel you come for the first time as my old lady on my cock."

His declaration was so damn romantic to me—butterflies swirled in my belly even as my pussy walls clenched again. Then he moved his mouth to mine, kissing me deeply so I could taste my own salty sweetness on my tongue. Something I didn't think I'd be into, but when it was Maverick, everything was perfect.

I gripped his shirt, making quick work of stripping him of his cut and flannel, only breaking the kiss to get rid of his clothes and then running my fingers down the hard lines of his chest and abs. I had come to know every black line of the tattoos on his chest. Even with my eyes closed, I had them memorized and ingrained in my memory like the feel of his body against mine.

Once his jeans were gone, his hard cock pressing against my stomach, his hands gripped my waist. Then he flipped onto his back, pulling me with him so I straddled his sides. I held on to his stomach, looking down as my wet folds met up with the head of his cock.

"Princess, do you know how beautiful this view is?" he murmured, tracing the hem of my vest and then up the freckles that dotted my stomach and chest.

"How does it look now?" I whispered, adjusting my hips and sinking onto his hard cock.

"Fucking amazing. Do you see it? How fucking hot you are with my cock inside you?"

I looked down where our bodies connected, the silver of my hood piercing a glint against his cock as I slowly slid up and down the length, my wetness coating every ridge.

"Is that how you ride, princess? Slow and steady?" His voice was thick as he rolled his hips to meet mine.

"You know I like to ride fast."

He grinned, his hands now gripping my ass.

By being on top, my clit hit his shaft at just the right angle, so every little movement shot a wave of pleasure straight through me. I knew it wouldn't take long to come, and I wanted to savor the moment.

But I also really, really wanted to come.

"Ride me. Hard and fast like the greedy little princess you are."

I gripped his chest, grinding my hips against his as I slammed my body against his cock over and over, feeling him pump in and out of me. Each movement sent little sparks of electricity through my entire body.

"I feel how wet you are, baby. Come over the edge with me. Now. Show me how you make yourself fly apart."

With one hand still firmly on his chest, I moved the other to my pussy lips. Circling over my clit with my thumb, I used my wetness to slide over his cock as I continued riding it.

"That's it, baby, fuck us both like the good girl you are."

My eyes slammed shut as I rode him harder, my entire body shaking as I threw my head back.

"Open your eyes," he growled.

I stopped moving, my eyes widening as I looked down at his face. He wasn't smiling or frowning, but something dark and wickedly sexy was in his eyes that sent a delicious shiver down my spine.

"You will look at me while I fuck you. I want to see your face when I fill you with my come."

"Yes, Maverick," I moaned, slowly moving my hips again.

He grinned, gripping my waist and rocking me harder. "I know you want it fast, princess. Come on, show me how good I make you feel. Come for me."

I rocked harder against him before circling my

clit again. Each little movement brought me closer and closer. But it wasn't until I really looked into Maverick's eyes. The way his hooded gaze locked on mine.

He was just as close as I was, and I wanted to go over the edge with him.

"You gonna come for me, Maverick? You gonna fill me up? Have me dripping with your come the rest of the day? Make it so everyone knows I'm your princess?"

"Fuck, yes," he growled, pumping his hips harder as I arched my back, taking every inch of his length.

"Right there. I'm gonna come, Mav. I'm gonna come," I cried as I finally found my release.

Fireworks spread through my body as I cried out, riding out my orgasm, my entire being convulsing over Maverick. He pumped hard and fast, moaning as he poured his hot come into me, not stopping until I'd milked every drop of him.

I was still coming down from my orgasm when he pulled me closer, kissing me fiercely as if his lips could say what words couldn't. How explosive our sex was. How, just from a kiss, I was ready for him to fill me again.

Then he rolled me over, his dick slipping out of

me as our mixed arousal leaked out of me and onto his sheets. His fingers were on my pussy, pumping in not one but two, already building me to the brink again.

"Keep that come inside you, baby. I want you full of me. Now come on my fingers again so I can feel you," he murmured before his lips trailed to my nipple, giving my piercing a tug with his teeth.

I bucked my hips forward, my already sensitive core still tingling. It didn't take long before I was rocking out another orgasm, screaming out his name as I shook around his hand.

"That's my greedy girl."

My eyes fluttered as I looked up at him, my body now sore like I'd just run a marathon.

Or rode one on his cock.

"Stay right here, princess," he commanded before hopping up, giving me a spectacular view of his naked ass as he walked over to the attached bathroom.

He quickly emerged again with a washcloth and gently cleaned between my thighs and my legs before tossing the washcloth somewhere on the floor with our discarded clothes.

"Tired?"

I nodded, my eyelids so heavy.

He lay down next to me, pulling the covers tight around us as I nestled against his chest.

As I felt his heart still beating heavily, my eyes fluttered closed. This was exactly where I belonged, and there was no way in hell I was ever going anywhere again.

Unfortunately, my dad wasn't going to easily agree with that plan...and had awful timing because he chose to call Maverick's cell just as I was drifting off. Although, it would've been a hell of a lot worse if it'd been five minutes earlier.

Maverick kissed my shoulder. "Sorry, princess, but I gotta answer."

Heaving a deep sigh, I nodded. "I know."

Twisting around, he bent down to lift his jeans off the floor and grabbed his phone from the pocket. Dropping them back down, he jabbed his finger against the screen. "Yeah?"

All I could hear was the deep murmur of my dad's voice, the words indecipherable but the tone obviously angry. Maverick let him have his say before his gaze met mine, determination blazing from his blue orbs. "I respect the fuck out of you, but coming for Molly isn't going to do you a lick of good, Mac. I'm not going to give her up for anyone or anything. She's mine now."

11

MAVERICK

W e were only a two-hour ride from the Silver Saints compound, but when Mac called, he was headed back from a run. He wouldn't be able to get here for at least half a day. Which meant I had a little time to figure out exactly how to handle this shit. Killing my old lady's dad wasn't an option but neither was letting her go.

A quiet knock on my door brought me out of my thoughts, and I carefully shifted Molly off my chest so I could get out of bed without waking her. She'd been worrying after the phone call with her dad, so I'd fucked her again until she passed out from exhaustion.

After pulling on a pair of boxers, I opened my

door to see Fox waiting in the hall, his expression grim. "Found him."

"Give me twenty."

Fox nodded. "My office." Then he stalked off.

I shut the door as quietly as I could, but when I turned around, Molly was sitting in bed, watching me with sleepy green orbs. Her hair was a disheveled mess, hanging in a riot of curls all around her, standing out starkly against her creamy skin and the white sheet she held over her chest. "Was that about my dad?" she queried, a frown marring her forehead.

"No. Why don't you get some more sleep, princess? I have to go meet with prez."

She shrugged and scooted to the edge of the bed. "I'm not tired. I think I'll see if I can scrounge up something to eat in the kitchen."

"Sure, baby. How about you shower with me first?"

Molly smirked. "Don't you have to meet with Fox?"

"It's just a quick shower."

Her expression was dubious. "That's what you said last time."

I grinned remembering just how that shower had gone. I'd made sure she was plenty clean...after dirtying her up and giving her two orgasms first.

"BE BACK SOON," I murmured to Molly, placing a kiss on her temple before leaving her at the entrance to the kitchen.

Fox was sitting behind his desk when I arrived at his office. He was talking with Whiskey who sat in a chair on the other side, and Deviant, Hawk, and Racer—three of our enforcers—and our officer, Midnight, sprawled in seats that surrounded a round wooden table in the right corner of the room.

We had a lot of meetings in this space, so it was large and also included a bar and lounge area with a couple of sofas. My office was connected with a door on the same wall as the table and looked very similar.

"Please tell me I get to kill someone today," I growled as I stalked into the room. I needed to take out my frustration at being pulled away from Molly again, and this punk seemed like the perfect target. Nobody messed with my woman.

Fox frowned. "I get your anger and need for revenge, but the little shit hasn't threatened Molly, so you'll probably have to settle for putting him in the hospital."

I shrugged, not happy with that option but settling for it. "Who is he?"

"Fritz Beals. Molly's first appointment the day you brought her to the shop," Whiskey answered. "He paid cash for the shit he sent her. But when word got around that we were looking, the florist told her man her suspicions, who brought them to Racer at the track."

"She sent him with her security tapes, and Whiskey recognized him," Fox added. "The fucker used a fake name for his appointment, but Hawk did some digging. Turns out, this isn't his first obsession."

"How the fuck did he get anywhere near my woman?" I bellowed at Whiskey, clenching my fists at my sides. I was still pissed as fuck at him for not telling me about the stalker in the first place.

"We can't run a background check on every customer, Mav," he grumbled, looking more irritated than usual.

"Why the fuck—"

"Uh, prez? Sorry to interrupt, but..."

We all turned our heads to see Jake standing in the doorway, looking nervous.

"Spit it out, prospect," Midnight growled, glaring at the prospect. One of the officer's jobs was to monitor prospects and their progress, so Jake paled at Midnight's gruff tone.

"There's a situation out front...some chick just

drove up to the gate and is demanding to see Mav's woman."

My brow furrowed. The only women who even knew Molly was here were her mom and sister. I didn't think her mom would go around her old man like that, so it had to be Dahlia.

"Let her in," I sighed, then looked at the prez and jerked my chin at the door. "I'll take care of it. Then we go have a chat with the motherfucker stalking my woman."

He nodded. "Get her the fuck out of here, Mav," he grunted. "Don't need any more shit piled on top of the situation with Mac."

I pivoted and stomped out of the office, entering the lounge just as Molly came running out of the kitchen, heading straight for the front door.

"Molly!" I shouted as I quickly followed her. She should know better than to run into an unknown situation. I was gonna put her over my knee and spank her ass later.

"It's just Dahlia," she called, throwing me a grin over her shoulder before disappearing outside.

"Fuck," I muttered.

The other redhead from Silver Ink was exiting a silver Mustang convertible, her anxious gaze seeking out her sister.

Molly slowed down as she approached Dahlia, probably due to her anxious expression.

"I can't stay," Dahlia said when Molly was a few feet away. "Dad is on his way here."

Molly sighed when she reached her sister and pulled her in for a hug. "I appreciate the warning, Dahls, but I already knew he was on his way. You shouldn't have come. Dad's gonna lock you in a freaking tower if he finds you here."

"I had to make sure."

Molly held Dahlia out at arm's length and studied her for a minute. Then she shook her head. "You also wanted to get out from under Dad's thumb, didn't you?"

Dahlia winced. "I swear, it was mostly about warning you, but since he's already pissed at me for covering for you, I'm gonna take off and meet some friends in Europe for the summer."

Molly laughed and was about to say something else when a man raced up the driveway from the compound gate and ran straight toward my woman.

He beat me to her by seconds, but I skidded to a halt when the sun glinted off metal, and I saw the gun he'd pressed to her temple. It was the little shit who was obsessed with her.

In the next second, I had my Glock pointed at his

head. "Let her go," I said in a deadly voice. "Can't say you're gonna leave here in good condition, but if you get your hands off my woman right the fuck now, you'll leave alive."

Fritz tightened his arm around Molly, making her gasp for breath. The punk's chances of getting out of this alive dwindled. "I'm going to walk right out of here, and nobody is going to touch me," he announced haughtily. "Molly and I are meant for each other, and nothing you do can stop us from being together. We love each other."

He looked behind me, and his smug expression slipped for a second. I had no doubt that my brothers had come outside and were at my back.

"Are you delusional, asshole? How the fuck do you think you're gonna get past us unscathed?"

"Because you won't hurt Molly," he answered, his tone slightly wobbly. "She and I are leaving, and if any of you attempt anything, I'll kill her."

My jaw clenched, but it was the only outward sign of my inner turmoil. I remained calm, almost detached, so he wouldn't realize that he had the upper hand as long as my woman had a gun to her head.

"You're signing you're own fucking death warrant."

He laughed somewhat maniacally and tightened his hold on Molly again, clearly causing her pain because tears welled in her eyes. I was proud of her for not showing any signs of fear, though, and for not attempting to save herself. She'd been taught how to defend herself, but she wasn't stupid. Her best chance was to trust me and my brothers, and she knew it.

"Why would you kill her if you love her?" Fox snapped as he stepped up beside me.

"If I can't have her, no one can," he replied with a shrug.

A movement out of the corner of my eye drew my attention. I frowned when I saw Dahlia—who was slightly behind Fritz and out of his line of vision —creep a few steps closer to him.

I pressed my lips together, swallowing the need to order her to stay the fuck out of this.

"I got it," Fox murmured, then he raised his voice. "I'm gonna open the gate for you." Slowly, he took a few steps, watching Fritz closely to see if he would let him pass.

Fritz nodded, his smug air firmly back in place. "You do that. Now, Molly and I are going to walk out to my car, nice and slow. Don't make any sudden moves, or I'll kill her."

Dahlia was focused on the stalker, so she didn't notice Fox come up behind her. His hand was over her mouth before she could make a sound, and he dragged her back to the driveway and around her car so she was shielded from the situation.

"There's nowhere you can go that we won't track your ass down and feed you a bullet," Whiskey snarled from my left.

The distinctive roar of a Harley engine drowned out Fritz's response and stole his focus. The second his eyes left me, I pulled the trigger.

The force of the bullet sent him reeling backward, and his heavy grip on Molly took her down with him. But the hand holding his pistol fell to his side, out of harm's way.

"Molly!" My gaze swung in the direction of the newcomer, and I recognized Mac Mackenzie as he roared his daughter's name.

I didn't give him another thought. Molly was my only concern. Tucking my gun into the back of my pants, I ran toward her. Mac reached her first and held out his hand and helped her up.

"Don't fucking touch her," I growled.

I didn't care if it was her fucking father. I was still reeling from the fear of losing the most important person in my life. The thought of anyone's hands on her but mine sent me into a blind fury.

Molly didn't even look at her dad. Her eyes were glued to mine, and she immediately released his hand before running the rest of the way to me and throwing herself into my arms.

"It's okay, princess. I've got you," Maverick murmured, stroking his palm down my spine.

I knew he'd been worried about the guy who'd sent me the flowers and stuff, but I'd just thought of him as a secret admirer. Not an actual stalker. I couldn't have been more wrong and had almost paid for it with my life. "If you hadn't been here..."

"You still would've been fine because my brothers would have made sure of it," he growled, pressing me closer. "There couldn't have been any other outcome. I can't imagine my world without you in it. Nothing is ever gonna happen to you."

"Fucking hell."

My head jerked up at the familiar, deep voice. I couldn't believe I'd forgotten that my dad was here.

"Daddy," I whispered, stepping away from Maverick to hug him.

His arms tightened around me as he rasped, "Shit. Fuck. Damn."

"I know you came here because you're not happy about me being with Maverick and were probably planning to try to drag me away from him, so I'm not super happy about that. But thank goodness for your timing because that could've been so bad if you hadn't distracted my...my...stalker," I babbled, tears streaming down my cheeks now that what had just happened was actually sinking in.

"You would've figured something out." My dad brushed a kiss against the top of my head. "All those self-defense lessons the guys and I have given you over the years would have kicked in, and you would have found your chance and gotten away from the bastard."

"Maybe," I mumbled against his chest. "I heard your voice in my head the whole time, telling me to stay calm and not let my fear rule my decisions. To bide my time for the perfect opportunity."

"So fucking proud of you, kiddo." He patted me on the back. "Even with a gun to your head, you didn't panic."

"I knew Maverick would do whatever it took to make sure I was okay."

"Yeah, I caught that." I tilted my head back, but my dad's gaze was locked over my head. "You're not good enough for her."

Pushing away from him, I heaved a deep sigh. "Seriously, Dad? Maverick just saved my life, and that's the first thing you want to say to him?"

Maverick came to my side and wrapped his arm around my back. "Don't worry, princess. I get where he's coming from."

I tilted my head back to gawk at him. "You just killed someone for me, and you don't care that my dad is giving you a hard time about being with me instead of thanking you for what you had to do to keep me safe?"

"I don't need your dad's gratitude." Cupping my cheek, he brushed his thumb over my bottom lip. "You standing here without a scratch on your perfect body is the only thing I need."

"You got my gratitude anyway," my dad muttered. "But it doesn't change the fact that you're not good enough for my daughter."

Maverick's hand clenched my waist as he replied, "I know, but she's mine anyway."

"I respect that because I've never been good

enough for her mother either." He speared Maverick with a hard look. "But I love the fuck outta my woman. Can you say the same about Molly?"

Before he could answer, I slammed my hand over Maverick's mouth. "Nope. You're not going to use that particular four-letter word for the first time while talking to my dad. If you want to make a declaration like that, it's gonna be aimed my way."

"You let him claim you without knowing if he loves you?" my dad growled.

"I let him claim me because I lo—" Pressing my lips together, I barely stopped myself from declaring my feelings for Maverick to my dad instead of him. "You can't be surprised by how things are going down in my relationship. Not when you've cheered on your club brothers as they've claimed their women pretty much the same damn way that Maverick did with me."

"It's different," he insisted. "None of them are my daughters."

I huffed out an irritated breath. "The double standard is so ridiculous. And frustrating."

"There's no 'if' about it, princess," Maverick murmured when I dropped my arm back to my side.

I twisted my neck to stare up at him, my brows drawing together. "What?"

"You said that I needed to give the words to you...if I felt them," he explained, tangling my hair in his fist to keep my head tilted back. "You gotta know there isn't a single doubt in my mind about how I feel about you, princess."

My breath caught in my throat at the emotion shining from his blue orbs. "There isn't?"

"Never believed in love at first sight. Thought it was a bunch of romantic bullshit before I met you." He brushed his lips over mine and rasped, "Felt as though I was hit by a bolt of fucking lightning. Straight to the heart."

"It was the same for me," I whispered.

"Shoulda told you before I left, no matter how little time we'd had together. I love the fuck out of you, Molly Mackenzie."

My heart was racing as fast as it'd been when that gun had been held to my head. But not from fear this time. It was because I was getting everything I'd ever wished for. "I love you, too. So, so much."

"Thank fuck." He claimed my mouth in a deep kiss, uncaring who was watching. Our tongues tangled together as he stole my very breath from me, leaving me in a sensual fog when he finally lifted his head again. "Never gonna let you go, princess. You're mine. All mine."

"Then I guess it's a good thing I wasn't planning on going anywhere." I smoothed my hands down his chest. "Because I'm never letting you go, either."

"Love seeing my property patch on you." Maverick stroked his hand over the leather vest that meant so much to me. Then he slid his palm down my arm to capture my left hand. Lifting it, he pressed a kiss to my ring finger. "But I want you to have my last name too."

Grinning up at him, I tilted my head to the side. "Is that your way of proposing? Because you missed a couple of things. Like a ring. And actually asking me."

"And getting my permission," my dad muttered.

"Wasn't planning on asking since it's a done deal, and I don't care about your dad's permission unless it matters to you." Maverick slipped his hand into a pocket on the inside of his cut and pulled out a diamond solitaire. "But I do have a ring."

"It's perfect," I sniffled.

"Just like you are." He slid the platinum band onto my finger before claiming my mouth in another deep kiss.

"I'm starting to think you don't give a single fuck that I'm standing right here," my father griped.

I beamed a smile at him. "Consider it payback

for all of the times you practically made out with Mom in front of me, which was like every day of my life."

He shook his head with a sigh. "You really love him?"

I nodded. "As much as Mom loves you."

"Shit," he groaned, stroking his hand over his beard as he eyed Maverick. "Then I guess the tie between the Silver Saints and the Iron Rogues is gonna get a fuck of a lot closer. But all bets are off if he hurts you."

"That's never gonna happen," Maverick swore.

"It better not," Dad warned.

"If it does, I'll take care of it myself." I winked at my dad. "Just like you taught me."

"Shoulda known all those lessons would come back to bite me in the ass someday." My dad chuckled. "Made you so damn sassy, you weren't afraid to ride off on the back of Maverick's hog. And your sister didn't hesitate to cover for you. I'm gonna have to keep a closer eye on Callie to make sure she isn't hiding any shit from me too."

I quirked a brow at him. "Maybe Dane is the one you should be keeping an eye on?"

"Right now, Dahlia is the one worrying me. Where the hell did she go?" Dad growled, his gaze scanning the area. "She should be back home, but I saw her Mustang when I pulled up."

Remembering what my sister had said about heading to Europe, I figured she took off as soon as she knew I was okay since she wouldn't have been able to make her escape otherwise. Not with Dad here.

Maverick chuckled. "You sure? I don't see it now. Don't see Fox either, and he was here a moment ago too, now that I think about it."

My dad scrubbed his hands down his face. "Fucking hell."

All of my focus had been on Maverick and my stalker when everything went down, so I hadn't seen Fox. But if he'd gone after Dahlia when she left, he would have one hell of a chase on his hands.

EPILOGUE
MAVERICK

"That's it, baby," I groaned. "Fuck yourself on my cock."

"Yessss. Oh, Maverick. Yes!" Molly dropped her head back, moaning as she rose and fell on my dick. Her tits bounced, and I tugged her nipple ring while my other hand caressed her swollen belly.

It was hot as hell to fuck my woman with the proof of my claim right in front of me. My palms traveled up her sides to cup her tits, gently squeezing the mounds that had grown even bigger since I put my baby in her.

Molly dropped down hard, and I frowned. "Careful, princess." The doctor had said there was no need to change anything about our sex life, but my cock was huge, and she was just so damn tiny. I knew she could take me, but I couldn't help worrying about hurting her or letting her over-exhaust herself.

"I need it harder," she whimpered, her movements growing rougher as she rode me.

I slapped her ass hard, making her gasp from a mixture of pain and lust. "Don't defy me, Molly, or you won't be able to sit down for a fucking week."

Her green orbs met mine, flaring with even more heat as she clenched her inner muscles, and I nearly lost control. "You want it hard, baby?"

She nodded frantically, but I grasped her hips to keep her from moving, smiling wickedly when she cried out, "No! Please, don't stop!"

"I'm just getting started," I told her before flipping us so she was on her back and pushed her legs open as wide as they could comfortably go. Then I bent her knees, planting her feet flat on the mattress.

Bending over her, careful not to put pressure on her stomach, I captured her mouth in a deep kiss while guiding her arms up over her head. My hips began moving, slowly at first, making sure to press on her piercing with each thrust.

She tore her lips from mine and whimpered desperately, "Maverick. That's so good. Oh, yes." Then she begged. "More. Please, Mav, fuck me!"

I only let her use that word when we were in bed

together because it awoke something primal in me. "You want me to fuck you, princess?" I wrapped her fingers around the headboard before sliding my hands under her ass. Then I pounded her like a man possessed...because that's what I was. She owned every part of me.

"Fuck, baby! Oh, fuck. Such a good girl, taking my cock so damn deep. Oh, fuck yeah. Fuck!"

"I'm so close," she panted, arching her back and thrusting her pelvis up to meet me every time I drove home.

"Come, Molly. Want to feel your pussy sucking my cock, milking me so I fill you full of me."

"Maverick!" she screamed as her orgasm crashed over her and her channel clamped down tight on my dick. The spasms of her climax rippled around me, and I slammed into her three more times before sinking as deep as possible. Then I roared her name, shooting my load over and over until she was so full it was oozing out between us.

When my shudders subsided and the world stopped spinning, I collapsed next to my wife and tucked her into my side. "Love you, princess," I murmured, tucking a few strands of her red curls behind her ear.

"I love you, too, Mav," she whispered sleepily.

Shifting our positions so we were on our sides, with her back pressed to my front, I splayed my hand on her baby bump and closed my eyes.

I'd been on club business for the past twenty-four hours and had pushed hard to get home as soon as possible. Missed the fuck outta my woman, and the moment I saw her, my only focus had been getting inside her.

Tomorrow, I had plans for us, but tonight, I was gonna rest, content to have Molly in my arms.

———

"You...YOU'RE going to build me a house?" Molly gasped.

I stood behind my woman, my hand resting on her belly and my chin on the top of her head. "Do you like it?" We had a lot of undeveloped land in the Iron Rogues territory, so I'd purchased a lot and decided to surprise my wife. I didn't want our baby girl living at the clubhouse, and I wasn't a fan of an apartment where the neighbors might hear my old lady's passionate screams. "We can look for a different lot if you don't. I picked it because it's close enough for you to walk to the studio but big enough to have a big backyard for our kids to play in."

"It's perfect." She turned and locked her arms around my neck, gazing up at me with so much love that it made my chest tighten. Then she frowned, but there was a twinkle in her eyes that told me she was about to get sassy. "Kids? As in plural?"

"I'm thinking four…maybe six…"

Molly's brow rose. "I assume you're expecting me to be the one to pop out those six—"

"Or eight…" I mused, cutting her off and swallowing a teasing smile. "You look so fucking hot carrying my baby, princess. Expect to be knocked up for the foreseeable future."

She gasped and stepped back, planting her hands on her curvy hips. "You cannot be serious! If you think you're going to convince me to have eight kids, you have lost your freaking mind!"

I grinned and tugged her back into my arms, plastering her body against mine. My dick never fully went down around my woman, but all this talk about knocking her up—even when she was currently pregnant—had me hard as a rock. I pushed my hips against hers and dropped my head down to lick a sensitive spot under her ear. "Is that a challenge, princess?"

"No," she sputtered, knowing I could get her to

promise me just about anything when my head was between her sexy thighs.

Laughing, I slipped my arm around her waist and guided her over to the SUV I bought the day after we found out she was pregnant.

I would never force her into anything she didn't want to do. If she wanted to be done after having our little girl, I would agree. But I was still gonna have fun trying to convince her.

"We'll figure it out when the time comes, princess," I told her as I helped her into her seat. Then I kissed the tip of her nose and smirked. "Until then, I'll just have to practice my powers of persuasion."

EPILOGUE

MOLLY

The birthday parties we threw for our children had always been more than a little over the top, probably because of the nostalgia since that was how Maverick and I had met. But this one was a little wild, even for us.

"Having fun, princess?" Maverick asked, coming up behind me and pulling my back against his chest as he wrapped his arm around my stomach.

"How could I not be?" I gestured toward all of the party rentals surrounding us. "We have bounce houses galore, cotton candy, shaved ice with a million flavor options, a taco truck, an entire petting zoo, and carnival games. There's something for everyone."

He chuckled, his breath hot against my neck and sending a shiver down my spine. "I probably should've forced Chase to make up his mind when he tossed out so many ideas for his party. It's a literal zoo around here."

We were surrounded by shrieking kids—a few of them ours—and a ton of bikers and their old ladies. Everyone was having a blast celebrating our son's sixth birthday. I had never seen Chase happier, and we hadn't even gotten to presents yet.

"We should do the cake soon, then gifts," I suggested.

"Sure thing, princess." Maverick squeezed me and brushed a kiss against the top of my head. "I'll go round up the kids if you want to grab the cake."

"Will do."

I headed inside the clubhouse—which had changed so much over the years as our Iron Rogues family grew by leaps and bounds. It reminded me more of the Silver Saints clubhouse than the place I'd walked into so many years ago after Maverick had brought me here. It'd been inevitable with so many of his club brothers claiming their old ladies and having babies.

I stuck six candles into the dinosaur cake and lit them, then walked outside to sing and watch my boy blow them out. There was a whole table full of other desserts—plus the cotton candy and flavored ices—

but that didn't stop us from devouring the chocolate fudge cake with green icing. When that was done and the table where Chase sat was cleared, Maverick and a few of the guys brought out the presents.

Chase tore into the wrapping paper, tossing it over his shoulder as he exclaimed over each gift. I thought we had saved ours for last, but after he opened the new game system he'd been begging for, my brother called, "There's one more from your aunt and me."

Heaving a deep sigh, I pinched the bridge of my nose between my index finger and thumb as I watched him roll a mini, gas-powered bike toward us. It was the other gift Chase had asked for, but we'd decided to hold off for at least another year since he wasn't old enough yet. But only because I'd resorted to sexual bribery to get Maverick to agree with my decision.

"Awesome," Chase cried, jumping out of his seat to run over to his uncle. "Is there gas in it? I wanna go for a ride!"

Crossing my arms over my chest, I tapped my foot on the ground and shook my head. "Nope. Absolutely not."

The bike my brother had gotten for my son was

adorable, but there was no way I would let him ride it right now. No matter how much he pouted.

"Aw," Chase grumbled.

"C'mon, sis. Don't be a spoilsport," Dane complained. "Chase is big for his age, and he's been on the back of Maverick's bike a ton of times."

"Don't worry, princess. I'll keep a close eye on him. He'll be fine," my husband reassured me.

"Only if Luna gets to ride too. Since she's actually old enough for the damn thing if we go by the age listed on the box that I'm sure my brother purposely didn't keep it in because he didn't want me to see it," I insisted, glaring at Dane.

"Fuck," Maverick groaned, raking his fingers through his thick hair.

"So now you're worried?" I asked. "If it's safe enough for Chase to ride when he's only six, then it's safe enough for Luna. "

Dane shook his head. "I can't believe you're still harping on about that double standard shit when we're all grown up with children of our own."

"That's easy for you to say when Dad got you a motorcycle for your sixteenth birthday, but Dahlia and I had to take riding lessons behind his back," I retorted.

Our dad crouched in front of Luna and asked,

"Do you want to go for a spin on your brother's mini-bike, sweetheart? Or would you rather go for a ride on Grandpa's motorcycle?"

"Sorry, Mommy." Luna flashed me an apologetic smile as she slid her palm against my dad's. "I'm gonna go for a ride with Grandpa."

"Me too," Aurora cried.

I glared at my father as he led my daughters away, and then heaved another sigh when I looked at my son's crestfallen face. "Fine, you can ride your uncle's present. But you're going to wear a helmet and elbow and knee pads."

"Yay," he cheered, not minding my rules as long as it meant that he got what he wanted.

I wagged my finger at him. "But your sister gets to ride it later if she wants."

"Sure," he quickly agreed, which wasn't a surprise since all of the kids were good about sharing their toys with each other. Even their favorites.

As Dane showed him how the mini bike worked, Maverick pulled me in for a hug. "Look how happy he is. You just made his whole day, princess."

"Yeah, well...keep today in mind when Luna wants to date, and everything in your body is screaming to say no," I warned. "Because the rules for our girls are gonna be the same as the boys."

"Fuuuuuck," he groaned, making me grin.

It was probably a good thing for Maverick that he hadn't given me the eight babies he'd talked about so many years ago...or else odds were good he'd have even more daughters to lose his mind over than the two that sandwiched Chase by a couple of years in either direction.

Want to know what happens with Fox and Dahlia? Find out in Fox!

In the mood for another age gap romance? If you join our newsletter, we'll send you a FREE ebook copy of The Virgin's Guardian, which was banned on Amazon!

ABOUT THE AUTHOR

The writing duo of Elle Christensen and Rochelle Paige team up under the *USA Today* bestselling Fiona Davenport pen name to bring you sexy, insta-love stories filled with alpha males. If you want a quick & dirty read with a guaranteed happily ever after, then give Fiona Davenport a try!

For all the STEAMY news about Fiona's upcoming releases... sign up for our newsletter!

Printed in Great Britain
by Amazon